I'm Not Hungry But I Could Eat

But I Could Eat

Stories

Christopher Gonzalez

sfwp.com

Advance Praise

With these stories of dance floors and Lyft rides, of afterparty bodega sandwiches, of self-loathing mixed with shocking vulnerability, topped off by moments of self-discovery, Christopher Gonzalez's writing will feed you.
— Tomas Moniz, author of *Big Familia*

The stories in *I'm Not Hungry but I Could Eat* are funny, tender, beautiful, and vulnerable. It is a collection that you immediately melt into as Gonzalez's gift is in the way he lures you in with the intimacy and sincerity of his voice. This collection is so important as it represents queer, specifically bi, yearning from a male perspective without the trappings of toxic masculinity and shows the depth and breadth of human emotions and the ways in which love, lonliness, and longing are complicated by self doubt. Everyone should read this collection!
— Tyrese Coleman, author of *How to Sit*

I'm Not Hungry but I Could Eat is a book about hunger, but not just food hunger. It's about the hunger of loneliness. The hunger of being the third wheel. The hunger of being unsure of one's place in the city or in love or in a crowded happy hour dive bar. These sharp stories, sometimes hilarious and sometimes wrenching, form a collaged portrait of longing and uncertainty. One thing, however, is certain: Christopher Gonzalez is a promising writer, and this is a compelling debut.
— Danny Caine, author of *Continental Breakfast* and *El Dorado Freddy's*, owner of the Raven Book Store

Few authors have the power to make readers feel seen at a visceral level, but Gonzalez achieves this in virtually every short story in this essential collection. His clear-eyed prose captures all the messy joys and crackling anxieties of modern queer life, inviting readers to join its Puerto Rican characters on journeys punctuated by desire, shame, and grace. *I'm Not Hungry but I Could Eat* is a stunning debut that will leave readers hoping Gonzalez has a long and fruitful career.

— Ruth Joffre, author of *Night Beast*

Christopher Gonzalez is a wholly original voice and this book is a treasure, crackling with real and important feelings. The stories of *I'm Not Hungry But I Could Eat* are funny, sharp and heartbreaking—and full of an enormous amount of hope.

— Jami Attenberg, Author of *All This Could Be Yours*

At times full of devastating portraits of bisexual Puerto Rican life, and at others full of the punchiest wit and charm, Gonzalez's writing leaves you insatiable…craving to need more and more from this exciting writer.

— Marcos Gonsalez, Author of *Pedro's Theory: Reimagining the Promised Land*

Gonzalez writes with such care and vulnerability. You feel the hunger in the text, a deference to the carnal that refuses easy categorization or shame. After you finish, you will need to eat.

— Raven Leilani, author of *Luster*

Names: Gonzalez, Christopher, 1992- author.
Title: I'm not hungry but I could eat : stories / Christopher Gonzalez.
Other titles: I am not hungry but I could eat
Description: Santa Fe : Santa Fe Writers Project, 2021. | Summary:
   "A compact short story collection about messy and hunger-fueled
   bisexual Puerto Rican men who strive to satisfy their cravings of
   the stomach, heart, and soul in a conflicted and unpredictable world"
   —Provided by publisher.
Identifiers: LCCN 2020054825 (print) | LCCN 2020054826 (ebook) |
   ISBN 9781951631215 (trade paperback) | ISBN 9781951631222 (ebook)
Subjects: LCSH: Puerto Ricans—Fiction. | Bisexual men—Fiction. |
   LCGFT: Short stories.
Classification: LCC PS3607.O558 I4 2021 (print) | LCC PS3607.O558 (ebook)
   | DDC 813/.6—dc23
LC record available at https://lccn.loc.gov/2020054825
LC ebook record available at https://lccn.loc.gov/2020054826

Published by SFWP
369 Montezuma Ave. #350
Santa Fe, NM 87501
(505) 428-9045
www.sfwp.com

Contents

For Erica

I'm right over here, why can't you see me?

—Robyn

There's no narrative to chicken tenders, there's no performance...
They ask nothing of you, and they don't say anything about you.
They are two things, and two things only: perfect, and delicious.

—Helen Rosner

Please note, every narrator and protagonist in this collection is a bisexual Puerto Rican cub with the exception of one—in that story, the narrator is gay.

Packed White Spaces

I'm riding the elevator up to Corinne and Allen's tenth-floor apartment with a bottle of $3.99 wine from TJ's tucked into my armpit. They are hosting a party to commemorate the purchase of their new Washer-Dryer unit, which I assumed was a joke when I read the Facebook invite, but nah, this is exactly the kind of dumb shit they like to do. They are my capital-W White friends who wear Sperrys and say "sketchy" to describe pre-gentrified neighborhoods, who live in one of the capital-N Nicest apartment units among our peers, because of Generational Wealth.

The Washer-Dryer lives in a nook next to the front door. When I enter, I bump into several guests gawking at the machine's sleek, stainless steel beauty. Allen is removing white leather pants from the Washer. A crowd bends forward, blocking my view; I'll say hello later, I guess.

I elbow my way past someone and they nearly drop their wine glass. Sorry, sorry, I say, excuse me, so sorry, and I hold my cheap wine high above my head like the visual beep-beep-beep of a semi-truck reversing, until I reach a break in the group. Around the room, I see a few familiar faces from college and a lot more strangers. Four years of an Elite Education and two seasons into a new phase of life—I still don't know how to navigate these packed white spaces. Not without Alejandra holding my hand. Not without Alejandra talking shit and laughing about everyone in the corner. I feel instant isolation. I'm all too aware of my presence, my casual clothes. How everyone is fitter than I am. In this space, I'm wondering if it's related to Money. Does Money have the power to stave off weight gain from fast-food dinners or a family history of diabetes? Does it cancel out the effect of a 2AM diner run for disco fries and syrup-drenched French toast?

Corinne stands in front of a Cheese Platter, not eating. She is all arms and perfume when she pulls me in for a hug, tight enough to collapse the last six months of distance between us. You made it, she says, then we're making small talk.

There's nothing interesting about catching up with a friend. Even a good one. I ask about work, and she asks about the movies I've seen, though I haven't yet gone to one since my move. The prices are so high I'm intimidated my experience won't match the cost. She wants to know how I'm enjoying my big New York City "adventure," which I loathe. "Adventure" is what white people use when they want their lives to sound spectacular. The truth is—it's all so mundane. I buy groceries. I sometimes eat them, I mostly let them rot. I go to work, then return home in the evening and pretend to sleep until it overtakes me. Wake up. Do it again. But Corinne is talking about Life and Vacation and Taking Out a Mortgage on the very apartment we're standing in. I shrug, smile when appropriate—I try to remember if we would have been friends without Alejandra introducing us.

I lob off a chunk of Parm with a Tiny Knife and laugh to myself. Corinne stops to ask what's so funny—she is in the middle of describing why she and Allen chose this specific model of Dryer, something about its high-heat, high-speed, high-efficiency—but it's not funny on its own to tell her that Alejandra once said it felt like the two of us were getting a full-ride to a Prestigious Liberal Arts College just to learn about the difference between Manchego and Mahón. Now, Alejandra's face and scent blooms in my memory and accelerates my heart rate. I ask Corinne if she's heard from her at all.

Oh, you know, we text, FaceTime every few weeks, she says. Her voice lilts, suggests *are we actually going to do this.* Not out of annoyance. She's feeling out if I can handle more good news about Alejandra. It was Corinne, after all, who had purchased the fine Champagne we drank to the point of blackout the night Alejandra and I kissed on the quad our junior year. She had been the most encouraging and excited for us. For *that* adventure. I unscrew my wine, nod my head to let her know it's okay. She's loving LA, Corinne says, and getting really into the activist community there. Crushing it, like we knew she would. What else can I say?

I, of course, know all of this. Alejandra and I are mutuals on Instagram and Twitter and still Facebook friends, though neither of us have posted anything there since graduation. I choose to recklessly scroll. I'm not being stalkerish, not intentionally, but the algorithm has a way of reminding me how much Alejandra loves her life. Her new boyfriend. Her new friends, Mexicans and Salvadorans and Puerto Ricans and Guatemalans, who all love to go out until 3AM on weekends and dance. So much dancing. She loves the mountains; she hikes now. Goes to the coffee shop in her neighborhood for an almond croissant every other day. My feed blinks alive with so much Alejandra content, always at the exact moment I'm doing something unimportant, like standing on the edge of a subway platform not fantasizing about death but wondering what it's like to be truly missed.

More people gather around the Washer-Dryer. Allen is at the center of the group, holding up the white leather pants. See, he's shouting, no damage. None! They're as good as new, even better. Steam rolls up from the pants, whirls around his face. A stench of dead cow fills the room.

High-power wash, Corinne says only to me, and one motherfucker of a heat setting. She winks, and I take a swig of wine. You'd think those pants would be ripped to shreds, she says. Hell, I've thrown in dresses. It blasts off the sweat and grime and leaves the fabric totally intact. How cool? Corinne puts on her creepiest smile and looks around at her other guests.

I'm a bit shaken at the sight of the pants, the cleanness of them. I spot-check my jeans and hoodie. There are probably stains I can't see. Sweat inside the legs, a ring around the collar. I feel hot with shame. I might pass out. I regret wearing this hoodie.

I ask Corinne where I might find the bathroom. There are no defined doors other than the front. All the walls, all the surface details are blindingly white. Minimalism at its worst.

Ah, Corinne says, that's the one thing I'd change about this place. She points into a dark hallway. The bathroom is through our bedroom. She then downs her wine and tells me to make myself at home. I mean it, she says.

Their bedroom is bathed in so much natural light I worry I've wandered outside. But, oh, what a view. They sleep in a King-sized Bed and own a Reading Chair, wedged in between two Oak Bookcases. I sit on the edge of the bed, drink more wine until my lips go dry. The Duvet Cover is Soft beneath my fingers. Wrinkle-free. Alejandra once told me that Allen fucks Corinne one way: doggy-style. It's the detail I come back to whenever I wonder why Allen and I never crossed the bridge from *friend's boyfriend* to *actual friend*. We shared a $200 Bottle of Macallan the night before graduation, but ask me, have I ever looked him in the eye?

The wall next to their bathroom door is adorned with eight Blown-up Photographs in Black Wooden Frames, spaced apart into a perfect grid. Scenes from their life that don't seem particularly noteworthy, but here they are, large, on display. I'm surprised by the inclusion of one from freshman year: Corinne, Allen, Alejandra and me soaked in our tie-dye t-shirts after serenading. I think I knew I liked her then. The attraction was immediate, but I didn't think it would become love. And how could

I know that it would break? I pull the Frame off the wall. There are tears in Alejandra's eyes, the kind that hit during late-night study sessions when we were consumed by blissful delirium. The Frame's backing is loose; I slide it off, remove the photo. I fold it in half, then in half again and again, and again once more until it's a compact little memory that fits inside my hoodie pocket. The blank space left behind on the wall is haunting, a violent gash. I'd swap in a different memory: the last time Alejandra and I laughed that hard together was shortly before the end, in a taxi headed back to school from the train station. I had been so drunk I kept telling the driver I loved him, he was a lifesaver, I loved him so fucking much. The snapshot doesn't exist, but it would look like this: Alejandra, her head out the window, howling into the wind.

After leaving the bedroom, a stranger backs into me and doesn't apologize. I drop my bottle, which shatters, and the wine splashes out with a mission, catches me good across my hoodie, like a bloodstain, a wound. The room goes horror-movie quiet. My instinct is to yell, to tell the guy who bumped into me to watch himself. I fight it. I don't want to be the angry brown guy in the room. Then Allen is at my side, hand on my shoulder, pulling at the hoodie.

It's all good, Allen says. This is perfect.

I'm struggling with the zipper. I fear he might break the fabric clean from the teeth. Everyone is watching. Allen says again, It's all good, then the hoodie is his. We're all here for a reason, right?

I'm left standing in a black shirt, pocked with holes. It's still a perfect fit, I'm convinced, not ruined enough to discard. I cross my arms over my chest, relieved when everyone turns away, and hurt that no one continues to stare.

Allen tosses the hoodie into the Washer's drum. Everyone gathers around to watch and I don't say anything. This will take less than five minutes, he says. Watch. Allen turns on the Washer and I still don't say anything. It fills with water quicker than any machine I've used. The fabric twists and turns over itself, into itself, becomes separate then whole. When the cycle ends, I push past Allen, grab my soppy hoodie, reach into the pocket. No photograph. The ink ran, streaks of tie-dye and hair and sunlight staining the inside of my pocket green and black. I climb into the drum. There's enough room for me to shut the door and die. I fish around, run my hands along the interior until I've gathered all the bits I can. When I back out into the room, Corinne hovers over me looking concerned. I ask her to open her hand, then I sprinkle the photo's wet remains into her palm, let them rain down in fat clumps. We can no longer make out the full picture, but the scraps, I tell her, the scraps are worth keeping.

A Mountain of Invertebrates

Austin orders an entire seafood boil for himself. He ignores the crawfish and halved cobs of corn, focusing instead on the crab legs, which he cracks open with such force the buttery juices mist Jorge's face. Jorge's plate is nearly empty now. He devoured his crispy-fried cod sandwich in five minutes, so he spends the rest of their meal together picking at coleslaw, catching only two or three strands of wet cabbage at a time on his fork. Austin finishes a fourth crab leg and leans back in his chair. He drapes a napkin over his lap. That was delightful, he says, but I can't eat another bite. Austin smiles at Jorge, his teeth flecked with parsley. You should try some, he says. But seafood is not Jorge's thing. The ocean, he believes, is swarming with aliens. No need to search for them in outer space when they lurk in the darkest depths of the earth. Certainly no reason to eat them. To roll the aquatic flesh around in his mouth would be an act against God. Hard pass, he thinks. But there is still so much shrimp and sausage and crawfish and potatoes cooling out on the newspapered tabletop. He imagines biting into the untouched crawfish, now: some uneasy chewing to start, then a rough swallow. Then, he suspects, the dead little fucker would be revived by the bath of his stomach acid. Reborn, it would swim down, deeper into his gut, burrowing itself within him forever. Jorge, come on, try it, Austin says again. Just one bite, please. He grabs a lobster from the pile, twists its body, and pulls until the tail separates from its torso. They could get a to-go container. There is still time. It's what other couples might do: wrap up the remains and tote the bounty back to Jorge's apartment, to be consumed in a post-sex haze. But that never happens, does it? Jorge knows Austin would leave the bag in his fridge as he had done with a slice of vodka pizza from their first date and the stuffed cabbage from date two and the Thai food from the third. The chocolate cake from date four never made it home. But for all those other leftovers, Jorge made sure to eat them. He was raised to be a garbage disposal. No waste, never. He picks over whatever Austin leaves in the mornings, shortly after Austin vanishes into the backseat of a Lyft. Off to class or work, Austin says. Alone in his kitchen, scraping his fork against an aluminum takeout container, Jorge watches the Lyft app every time, notes how the driver passes Austin's job, and the school, and even his apartment. Jorge watches Austin slip away, upstream. Austin is squeezing the lobster's torso now, and the red shell compresses under his fingers, cracking. Juice rains down over the newspaper. From the carnage, Austin presents Jorge with a lump of yellowish-green meat pulp, balanced delicately on his fingertips. That's it? Jorge laughs, he has to, everything feels too wild. So much effort and mess? All of that for so little? He's serious. He's confused. You'll see what all the fuss is about, Austin says. He swears it, raises the mass to Jorge's face. Jorge thinks about the bag of seafood, how it will surely sag, the paper thinning out over time, long after tonight, eventually breaking open all over his bottom shelf. Rancid garlic butter everywhere and a mountain of invertebrates decomposing. Jorge opens his mouth, welcomes Austin's fingers. He rolls the meat on his tongue, fights against the stinging in his eyes and rising bile in his throat, tries to push through. Austin is a wide smile and two celebratory balled fists. So good, right? he gasps. I knew you'd love it. But Jorge is still chewing the lobster, nodding his head over and over again. The hope is the movement will guide the sea bug down his throat and he can will himself into saying this thing is good. The hope is, it won't be a lie.

Better Than All That

I made the mistake of sitting next to Lucas at dinner. He spent the meal swiping through photos on his phone. After every fourth photo, he'd stop and nudge me with his elbow, and when I would give in and look down, I'd find a video clip of a woman fingering herself. "Damn, this shit is weak," he commented on one. "Is she kidding me with this?"

I looked around the Applebee's, locked eyes with a pig-tailed little girl sitting a table over from us. The crust of an onion ring dangled from her bottom front teeth; she draped its stringy skeleton over the lip of a ketchup-stained plate. "I don't know, Lucas, it looks like she's trying her best?" I offered.

"Absolutely she ain't," he said, then closed the video.

Across the table, Ray and Zeke sat in their own little world. One full of laughter, with Zeke's giggles helicoptering throughout the restaurant. It seemed that nothing had changed since high school. Although, now, Zeke drank. And he was drunk. And had been since 3PM, according to Lucas. It was a steady buzz.

But Ray's smile was the same, his teeth that perfect shade of yellow I find attractive. They looked soft to the touch. Even now, I still remember him from high school: skinny arms wrapped tightly around Alyssa, anxious she might float away like a balloon. I lost minutes staring at him, at both of them, if I'm being honest, when they kissed in public. I spent too many school nights alone in my bedroom with my body pressed up against the standing mirror. I leaned in timidly, mimicking the way Alyssa would receive Ray's kisses, until the cold glass warmed slick beneath my lips. This felt appropriate. Those early, nervous encounters between Ray and Alyssa were always so quick and stale, containing all the passion of a cold fish. I wish it stayed that way between them.

"Come on, man, let me have my phone," Ray said. His cheeks were rosy from the discount margarita mix. He extended his hand toward Zeke, who responded by tucking Ray's iPhone into the breast pocket of his suit.

"Not gonna happen, Ray-ray," Zeke said. "Can't have you sneaking a FaceTime session with Alyssa. It's my job to keep an eye on you."

"Yeah, Ray, one night apart won't kill you," I said, but when neither of them acknowledged my words, I returned to sipping a watery sangria through a cracked straw.

Then Lucas opened another video album on his phone. "Pay attention," he said only to me, hitting the play button. In the video, a faceless woman stood in a shower, sat on the edge of a bathroom sink, plucked her right nipple with dental floss, and then splayed her body out on a couch with a towel tucked underneath her ass. She played with herself for a while, her long-nailed fingers slipping in and out focus. Once she came, Lucas looked me right in the eyes and said, "See? That's effort."

I scratched my thumb. He shook his head at me and sucked his teeth. "What's with you?" He opened another video, consuming each new megabyte of footage with Rottweiler hunger. Why did he come out tonight? Surely, he'd rather slobber over the screen, alone, and use the excess drool as lube. The thought of him rubbing himself raw underneath the table ballooned in my mind and the back of my neck felt hot. I returned to my sangria.

I knew going into the evening things would get awkward. More than six years had passed since I last saw either Lucas or Zeke, whose faces had hardened, though neither in an unattractive way. I felt so boyish and plump seated next to them, as if all that time away had only held me back in their timelines. And then, Ray—I wanted to keep it going, our friendship. I swear I tried. I learned of his engagement soon after I moved back to Cleveland and started working at the main branch of the library downtown. Not the research gig I wanted, but a solid job at the circulation desk. I saw their faces on my phone while eating a desk lunch. I had prayed on many drunken, lonely nights in college and the years right after for their relationship to fizzle out. All that wishing and hoping proven a waste of time and spirit when I saw their large smiles, the blindingly white diamond. I never expected to receive an invite to the bachelor party. But, one day, Ray popped up in my DMs—"I'm getting married! Crazy, right? Saw you're back in town and I want the whole gang back together!"—and what could I say but yes?

After dinner, we hit up a bar in Ohio City. Zeke ordered everyone a round of shots; he requested Jameson, which he called "an honest whiskey for true gentlemen." The bartender set down four shot glasses. "What are you guys up to tonight?" His voice was smoother than I expected.

"We're here to celebrate our buddy Ray-ray's final nights as a single man," Zeke said. He adjusted the knot of his tie—he was the only one of us to dress up. "If the ladies ask, he's no longer on the market." And there it was again, Zeke's laughter clanking around the room.

"Oh, I wouldn't worry about any of that," the bartender said, topping off the last shot. "It's Boys' Night. Won't be a single woman in sight starting in about, oh, twenty minutes."

"Man, what?" Lucas said. He stood quickly, nearly knocking over two bar stools. "You didn't say nothing about no Boy's Night, Zeke, what kind of game do you think we're about to play?"

Whenever I'm overwhelmed with nerves, I feel my chest go concave, like a vacuum sucking me into another dimension. I can handle it, usually. It passes if I close my eyes, breathe. The real difficulty is with my hands—they flush cold and drip sweat. I gripped the bottom of my shirt to absorb the moisture and focused on Ray to see how he would handle the situation.

"Relax, big guy," the bartender said without yelling. "I was joking. No Boys' Night. It was a little joke is all."

Lucas wiped his mouth with the back of his hand before sitting down again. "Cool, cool. Better be." He disappeared into his phone.

"Hey," Ray said, taking his shot from the bartender. "Even if it was Boys' Night, it's not like we can't hang. Turn on 'Dancing Queen' and you know I'll be cutting it up with the rest of them." This was the right response. Ray had always been a peacemaker, his presence an oasis from all the toxicity I grew up with at home. He laughed and that made it OK for all of us to laugh.

The bartender, balling up a rag in his hands, rolled his eyes. No one else saw. It was a special moment between the two of us. I studied his face for a beat, perhaps a beat too long: his jawline was pronounced, and though his ears were perfect in size, one was blessed with an extra flap of skin sprouting from its lobe. Something clicked into place, then, and I felt that our two faces had exchanged this look before. That we had shared moments of understanding. Returning home was full of these brief encounters with former friends and newfound strangers, only this time, there was nowhere to hide, no department store in the mall to slip into, no unfollow button to click.

"Can I get you guys anything else?" the bartender asked.

I requested another round of shots, smiling as I said the words, hoping that Ray might see me, that he would catch me planning out the next step in our night. It was so easy to recalibrate my senses. The bartender nodded, said he'd hook us up after helping another group farther down the bar. I continued to study his face, then his body, how he walked. When he was out of earshot, I tapped Lucas on the shoulder and whispered, "Does the bartender look familiar to you?"

Lucas looked up from his phone. "So, what if he does?" He had opened his Snapchat, and with a tap of his thumb, a brief four-second video passed like a hiccup across his screen—what little I saw of the woman's face resembled a willow tree.

"Just an observation," I said, accepting a shot glass from Zeke. It felt sticky around the sides.

"I got an observation to make," Lucas snarled, and I remembered a time when he cried during gym after taking too many volleyballs to the face. His crying was guttural, painful. An exaggeration. "You need to get some pussy tonight," he finished. I blinked, searching his face for that little boy, my former friend.

"On that note," Zeke cut in, "I think it's about time we make a little toast. Tomorrow, Ray-ray, we say farewell to your life of being a loner. As you walk through the valley of the shadow of marriage, fear nothing, for your boys will always be around with a beer, a blunt, and a bulldozer to break you out of your matrimonial prison." Lucas and Zeke laughed at an upsetting volume. They swallowed their shots sloppily and slammed the glasses down. I was confused about the whole thing—why so much kicking and screaming when it comes to marriage? Unless Ray didn't want to marry Alyssa. Unless…there was hope.

Ray smiled and said nothing about the toast. He set down his shot glass, and a lovely daze melted his expression; the heaviness of his eyes held me in place. He pulled me in for a one-armed hug. "Justin, were you always this quiet?" The humidity inside the bar had bubbled up and Ray's skin was sticky with sweat. It smelled strongly of him, slightly soured from a weak cologne, and musty, like a room without windows. Too much like home. I inhaled deeply for a second or two too long. Being this close to Ray reminded me of all those sleepovers at his house where I failed to ever sleep. All those nights spent on an air mattress at the side of his bed. That's when we were at our closest. I reaped the benefits of being a guy, sharing an intimate space with him years before Alyssa ever could.

Ray jostled my shoulder a little. "Come on, man, nothing you want to add?" he said. "Or are you going to leave us hanging?"

"Oh, I don't know if there's anything I could add to"—I gestured toward Zeke—"I think all that needed to be said was said. And, speeches are kind of like masturbation, you know. Usually a solo thing."

"Jesus, just say something about him and Alyssa, you fool," Zeke said. He stood a good foot above my head, straightening his tie, but he wasn't looking at any of us. He was eyeing his own reflection in the mirrored-wall behind the bar. Licking two of his fingers, he smoothed out both eyebrows; a dot of spit sparkled near his left temple.

The longer I sat in silence, the closer Ray and Zeke hovered. Alyssa was a friend once, too, I needed to remind myself. I was hard-pressed to pull a good Alyssa story from my memory. We shared hand lotion in the back of twelfth grade English—that was something. She would slide the excess from her hands over my palms, which I welcomed, greedily, imagining which parts of Ray's body she had touched the night before.

"OK," I started. The three of them leaned in. "I'm really glad you invited me out tonight, Ray. And that you and Alyssa have stuck it out. The two of you make a cute pair." Impressed with my own lying abilities, I allowed myself to pat Ray's hairy arm, enjoy its softness on my fingertips. And if it had been just the two of us, the rest of the night might have played out more pleasantly, but there was Zeke again, cutting in with a "Check this fag out."

And then Lucas: "That's what I've been saying, man. Real talk." His laughter was at a twenty now. I wanted it to be at a negative three. "When you're not getting the pussy, you become one," he said. He and Zeke exchanged high-fives, the haunting sound of flesh against flesh. Zeke broke off into a little step-routine from his fraternity days at Akron University and palmed wildly at this thigh; he slammed each foot down with such intent I worried the tile would crack. Finished, he threw his head back and howled, stopping only when he exchanged eye contact with a redheaded woman sitting in front of a window. Other nearby women gasped. One said, "Ugh."

And Ray: he was cheesing, all teeth. This was not the right reaction. I felt an ache in my chest, a squeeze—after all this time, how stupid I was to keep pining after him, if only in my head, to continue fantasizing that Ray was mine.

"Come on, Zeke, really?"

"Here he goes," Lucas said to Zeke. "I warned y'all, didn't I? Homeboy acts like he wasn't talking mad shit himself every damn day through graduation."

I remembered the bartender then, felt a pull come from the other end of the bar. A sense that I should apologize for my former friends, their behavior, for a potential slight from the past, began to weave its way through my heart, but I was convinced that, even if I was once the shitty guy Lucas remembered, I was never as bad as them. I had left the state and met new, wonderful people who opened up the world beyond the four of us. I must have been *better*.

"Guys, guys, guys," Ray said, "this is my party and you're really bringing me down." I slid out from under Ray's arm. I hated how cold my neck got now that it was free. Ray stood, threw one arm each around Zeke and Lucas. The three of them appeared before me like giants, an impenetrable wall.

"You need to let Justin know then. Because he ain't better than us." Lucas turned to me. "Got that? You ain't better than us."

"Have another drink," Zeke said to Lucas. "It'll be chill."

I turned away from them and glanced up at the mirror, caught Zeke leaning closer to Lucas, mumbling, his hand placed firmly on

Lucas's chest to keep him from reaching forward and dragging me to the floor. If we fought, he'd win, but I would fight dirty. I could feel it in my fingertips, an itch to tear at his face. I folded my hands to calm them, and when my adrenaline lowered, I heard that word again: *fag*. A one-two punch of a word, but at least in the privacy of my invisible gay life, I tried to pretend like it would never hurt me. And anyway, I wasn't concerned about my own faggotry. After all, how could they really know for sure? It was the bartender. I got a vibe. I checked over my shoulder to find him snapping an orange peel against the edge of a highball glass. The festive lighting accentuated the slight crook in his nose and the fullness of his eyebrows, his cheeks and lips. I desired a kiss. Leaning closer to the bar, I wished to block out everything. I blinked, but it did nothing to erase Lucas, who had shifted gears and started making small talk with the redheaded woman, or Zeke, too occupied with dabbing at a spot of Jameson on his tie to notice Lucas had intercepted his potential date. And even Ray, both elbows on the bar, his back arched, unfazed by their vulgar behavior. I pictured all of them in another scene, another place, so I could observe the bartender, how at home he seemed.

When the bartender reappeared, I yelled my order—a Manhattan—too loudly. He laughed, and said, "You got it." After stirring the bitters, sweet vermouth, and whiskey together, he poured the contents into an icy glass and dropped in a cherry, which broke gracelessly through the drink's mahogany surface, sinking to the bottom. He pushed the cocktail forward. I allowed my hand to land on his for a second or two, and when there was no sign that either of us would be the first to pull away, I made direct eye contact. So strange and exciting to observe the watery nature of someone else's eyes, and to show them yours, dry and red-veined, as I'm sure mine were. My eyes have always lacked significant lubrication. Too many hours spent reading and staring at screens, following past timelines in real time. Locked in his line of vision, I felt a growing burn in my chest that we truly did know each other. I opened my mouth to ask if he remembered me, but Zeke slapped me on the shoulder, jerking me forward. The reality of the evening rushed back: Ray. I was here for Ray, at least for tonight. Not this familiar stranger, who was gone when I lifted my head.

Lucas's redheaded acquaintance, we learned, was named Maeve. She lured us to another bar that was much darker than the first. We drank low-priced margaritas with tequila levels so high the following morning promised a hangover, the kind that limps around the stomach like a bloated worm. The boldness of Maeve's hair dazzled me, the same fire engine red I'd dyed my own hair back in college. I immediately regretted the decision and went to a barber the next morning for a buzz cut, the red locks falling to the floor like confetti. For Maeve, the color was stunning. And maybe the drinks were hitting harder at that point, because I admired how easily she worked her way into the group. I envied her for it, for one or two seconds, then it disappeared.

Maeve spoke to the other guys about her history with using voodoo dolls to manipulate her twin brother into committing heinous acts for fun. She liked to get revenge and use him as a medium for execution. I don't believe in the supernatural; my attention dipped, then circled back to the bartender. I tried to refocus on Ray, reminded myself he was the reason I came out tonight, but across the table, Ray faded deeper into a drunken stupor, his head rolling back and forth on his shoulders. Looking at him no longer sparked joy. To avoid falling into the sadness of feeling drunk and alone, I focused instead on Lucas's hands, his fingers. I imagined him inserting one inside of me, brushing the tip of my nipple with the pasty stump of a thumb. I frowned at the unerotic possibility of such an encounter and realized with confidence that if Lucas were soliciting sloppy photos and dirty talk from me on Snapchat, I wouldn't push out my A-game either.

Maeve revealed her method for carving out the genitalia of voodoo dolls and Ray, who had been teetering in his seat, bolted from the table. He stumbled into the bathroom around the corner from my chair. We could hear his share of the nacho platter water-falling into a toilet bowl.

Zeke checked his watch nervously, not at all soberly. "It's not even one yet. Too early for him to be caving right now like a punk." He tilted forward, rested his head on his left shoulder.

"How are you still standing at all?" I asked. He belched in response.

"Just calling it now," Lucas said. "I'm not going to be the one to carry Ray back to the car." He said this while picking at the nacho debris, scraping at a chunk of solidified cheese and jalapeño with a nail.

"Why don't we have a little fun with him?" Maeve said, rising from her chair and slipping onto Lucas's lap.

There were whispers of a plan, one I was not able to hear, until Zeke finally yelled out, "Maeve, you're a genius!"

"Listen," he slurred, "our friend needs us, OK? Let's go pay Ray-ray a visit in the shitter and, uh, snap a few photos." He held onto the last syllable like a soccer commentator.

We found Ray in a puddle of limbs and sweat at the base of the toilet. He clutched his neck as if all that heaving risked decapitation. "Ugh," he mumbled. "God, no." A red light bulb swung two feet above his head casting a glow on the walls and mirror, highlighting an obscene amount of satanic graffiti.

"We should probably collect him," I said. "You know, get him home?" The night could end right there as far as I was concerned. I prayed for a last call, for the lights to turn up and wash us all in harsh yellows.

"I know what to do." Maeve pushed past me and closed the lid of the toilet. Ray flopped onto his side, against the tiled wall. "A little help, guys?" She dragged Ray closer to her. With Lucas's help, they hoisted Ray onto Maeve's lap; she cradled him like a baby, his head falling down into her chest. Maeve then lowered her top, freeing one of her nipples. She and Ray looked like Madonna and child.

"Here, you can use my phone," Zeke said. His face was doughy now after pounding too many cocktails. Once the phone was in my possession, he wedged himself deeper into the bathroom, down onto the small floor space next to Ray. At some point in the phone exchange, Lucas managed to fit himself into the tight space, too, and sat behind Maeve on his toilet tank throne.

"Come on, take the picture, dude," Lucas said. His eyes widened and he pointed to Maeve with his chin. The sooner we finished up here, the sooner the two of them could go off somewhere to screw. Lucas seemed to be living his life the way everyone else around me did. Coworkers and classmates, from Cleveland to Syracuse: everyone chasing the next fuck, stitching together love from reckless connections. I had saved my heart for Ray and missed out on a lot of living, other possible hurts. Now, his pathetic form was wrapped around the toilet, and I wondered how different this night would be, if it would exist at all, if I ever told him how in love—we can call it love—with him I was back in high school. If there was a small chance he might have felt the same way, too.

"Come on, my legs are falling asleep here. Take the picture!" Maeve yelled.

I believed I was holding Zeke's phone. Before opening the camera, I saw the background image: Alyssa and Ray, the two of them hugging behind a large, red birthday cake. A glob of frosting on Alyssa's nose, her entire face speckled with it. Ray's eyes almost gone from too much laughter. Both of them, mostly Alyssa, beaming like they had nothing else to live for but that moment. And the grin on her face, so sharp and cruel, mocking me now as she had years ago.

At the after-prom our senior year, a bad mix of Southern Comfort and Four Loko left me wobbly and too honest. Alyssa and I had been looking at a photo of her and Ray from the dance, and she asked me if it wasn't the cutest photo I had ever seen. Actually, what she said was, "This shit is cute as fuck, right?" And I said, "No, no, let me show you." After fumbling for quite some time, I pulled up a picture of Ray, Lucas, Zeke and me from our limo ride to Alyssa's house. I covered up Zeke's and Lucas's faces with my thumbs, told her this shit was the cutest.

I suppose I could blame my decision to come out to her on cheap alcohol and junk food. Throughout high school, I believed if Alyssa ever uncovered my desires, she would slap me, maybe even call me names, which would have been awful enough, but instead she laughed, nearly a bark, right in my face. "Justin, Justin, don't be ridiculous," she said. "Don't joke like that, what the fuck? Ray ain't gay." And I laughed back, tried to play it off, but a line had been crossed. She side-eyed me and attached herself to Ray, a cloak on his thin frame, for the rest of the night.

In the bathroom, I snapped a photo, then another. I stopped after the guys asked for a third. I suggested both Lucas and Zeke leave so I could get one with Maeve and the groom-to-be. Something passed over Lucas's eyes on his way out of the bathroom and he hesitated for a second, not stumbling out like Zeke. But whatever was on his mind didn't keep him too long. He squeezed past me, patting my back.

In the picture I took of just Ray and Maeve, Maeve's smile rivaled Alyssa's. I gave no thought to what came next—I sent it to Alyssa.

I joined the other guys outside the bathroom and said nothing as I tucked the phone back into Zeke's front pocket. He cocked his head at me like a confused bird, his hair just as feathered. Gone was the bowl haircut from junior high. Gone was the acne and the guy who once stayed home from school for three days in the seventh grade because his girlfriend dumped him in a note. He blinked and then the night's goals re-consumed him. "Another drink!" he declared to the group. Together, Lucas and Maeve shared the weight of Ray in their walk toward the bar. Ray's eyes were half-closed, narrow slits in which might have existed a drop of recognition. I watched the four of them overwhelm a short bartender with tropical drink orders and another demand for whiskey shots. Everything as it was. Like nothing significant had happened at all. Perfect timing to make an exit.

I walked for a bit, my inebriation dragging me down. Every footstep vibrated up my shin to the top of my knee. Any movement occurred both slowly and quickly, like I was existing between segments of time, trying to hold on to what came before and what was to come. I walked in this topsy-turvy manner for three blocks or so before I stopped to rest my shoulder against a brick wall.

A man, also leaning against the cold bricks, stood a foot away, smoking a cigarette. He extended it toward me, but I waved it off. I wanted to save all the moisture in my mouth.

"Never understood how you hung out with those guys," he said, taking an incredibly long drag. For a moment, I believed this man might save me. I asked him if he was God.

"I've gotten 'Adonis' before, but never a flat-out 'God.' I dig it." His head bobbed as he spoke, though not in a drunken way. He laughed, too, the soft, velvety chuckle of a man who knew more than he was letting on. There was enough light from a streetlamp cutting across the both of us for me to recognize an extra fold of skin on his ear.

"Wait, I know you."

"Ah, so you do. Thought you were looking at me funny." A few people passed by in groups of six and eight, all of them laughing. There was a bachelorette party across the street; all the women wore plastic penis necklaces, the bride in a hot pink veil. "You stare like no other," he said. "Don't worry, I won't tell your homeboys or anything like that."

I was the level of wasted where moments ago felt like last week. At some point, during my walk, the memory of my so-called friends began to blur into brown. All that mattered was the bartender standing in front of me. "Wait, though, so you remember me?"

"Remembered your friends first, to be truthful. That guy Zeke was always kind of a shit. But then I saw your face and I realized who you were. Man, oh man, if anyone from school had told me one day Justin Figueroa would be checking me out in a bar." He tucked his free hand into a pocket and inched closer to me. I flinched. He paused, stepped back. "Yeah, anyway," he said, peeling himself now completely from the wall. He flicked the cigarette out onto the street. "Guess I wasn't much on your radar back then."

"Oh, God, I wasn't a shit to you or anything, was I?"

He laughed, hard, from deep inside of his gut. "Oh, Justin." Then he folded his arms and smirked at me. "Not at all. You were one of the good ones. One might say, damn near perfect." He stepped closer and this time I didn't move. He raised his hand to my chin, stroked the stubble and leaned in, close enough to kiss. "The name's Xavier."

I swallowed hard and fiddled with the bottom of my shirt. "Xavier," I repeated. "I'm so happy I ran into you."

We chatted some more, the two of us standing outside a bar like friends. It felt like the right way to end this night.

He asked if I should be getting back to the others after we had been standing for quite some time, long enough for him to almost miss the end of his shift. It must have been after 2AM —the bars around us would be closing soon. I fumbled over myself to retrieve my phone, which had been silent the whole night. Since leaving the bar, I had received eight missed calls, three voicemails, twenty-seven text messages, and a Snapchat request from a user named RaveGirlMaeve39. My eyes watered from the bright screen. Xavier asked if everything was all right and I was quite sure nothing could ever be all right again. But the night would roll on. Tomorrow, another day. These are the things I told myself. I slipped the phone back into my pocket and asked, "Do you live close by?"

"There's not much in the way of food here, so if you're hungry we may have to order in. I think Nunzio's is still open. And I'm sure I got some booze around if you just want to drink." The fridge door opened and closed; Xavier rummaged through a cabinet over the sink. I tucked my knees to my chest and tried to concentrate on the sounds of his apartment: his movements, the whirr of his heater, the blood whooshing in my head, the meow-like flush of a toilet downstairs.

Xavier emerged from the kitchen with two glasses of a frothy white liquid, speckled with brown. "Coquito?" he offered. "It may be a year or so old, but alcohol doesn't really go bad."

I sipped the coquito, refusing to top off my night of heavy drinking with a glass of sugar. Xavier chugged his serving, pulling the glass from his lips to reveal a fleck of coconut saluting out from his gums.

"Cute," I said. A childhood of watching rom-coms in the privacy of my bedroom had a greater effect on me than I wanted—of course my dialogue was destined to be cheesy. What was I supposed to do? He smiled and, after wiping away the foamy mustache from his upper lip, he stroked my chin.

Then, without any of my usual complicated thinking, we were kissing.

I had spent all of college worrying that when I finally got to kiss a guy, Ray would still be heavy on my mind, like some permanent dent in my head. So many years of thinking about him, of hoping I might be with him, all those ways I had stretched to fit into his world. But maybe it's possible I actually was better than all that. Better than that guy I stowed away. Better than the group of friends I once thought I belonged to, but never truly did, who were growing increasingly sloppy and drunk in a city that once felt like home. Fuck it. Let Alyssa get mad at Ray. Let them experience a shift, a fracture that comes with seeing something outside your own reality.

When Xavier broke our kiss, he was shirtless and I was kicking off my boxers. He reached down to grab my pants from the floor, which he held momentarily, giggling. "Let's go out to my balcony," he said, and before waiting for him to stand, I was at the sliding glass door, my hand eager to pull it open, to get outside.

The kissing continued. Xavier's long fingers traced along the edge of my shoulders and arms, pausing somewhere at the base of my stomach. He gripped me tightly around my waist, quite hard, possibly bruising me, and when I winced, he switched to my shirt, which he yanked over my head and tossed back into his living room where the rest of my clothes lay scattered.

Completely naked, I stood on the balcony reaching hungrily for Xavier's belt. But he retreated, stepping back over the threshold. He lingered in the doorway, the tufts of hair on his chest tickled by a breeze swooping in between us.

"Wait," he said, "I just gotta look at you." I tried to smile at him flirtatiously, bit my bottom lip and focused on squinting my eyes just enough, the way I had seen Lucas do in a number of his Instagram selfies. Xavier pulled a phone from his back pocket and pointed it at me. "May I get a photo of this night?"

I laughed, folding my arms. There were parts of my body no one had seen before tonight. But when Xavier asked again, saying "Please?" I thought, what the hell? I struck a pose, the sexiest one I knew.

He snapped the photo then lowered the phone, tapping several buttons. I thought he was saving it. He continued for a second or two longer. "You know, I've never been able to forget you all these years," he said, the phone still bright on his face.

I teared up a bit. It was silly, I know. But someone was thinking about *me* for once. Someone was choosing to fit me into *their* memories. Maybe moving back home was the right thing to do.

Xavier smiled again. "To be honest," he said, "I thought about you a lot in school. And for years after. You were, how should I say this?"—he drummed his fingers along the phone—"An absolute monster." His laugh flopped out, all the warmth stripped away. Although I didn't try, I knew I wouldn't be able to walk. One foot in front of the other, a concept that now seemed foreign to my body.

"You won't remember this at all, now will you, Justin? But I recall you saying some shit to Ray about me once." A tree rustled in the backyard, the swishing leaves sounding like rain. I was twelve, or maybe thirteen when I started to feel for Ray, thinking and dreaming about him whenever we were apart. Lucas once asked why I spent every gym class staring at Ray. It had been his sweatpants. But I wasn't the only one, and as Xavier spoke, it all came back: trying to catch sight of his dick flapping inside the fabric. "You were just making sure I didn't do anything gay, huh, Justin? Worried that faggy Xavier might try something with him, and you were just looking out, right? Your boys may be scum, Justin, but so are you."

The phone hit my chest harder than I expected. I fell to the floor, extending my hand to catch it before it could shatter on the porch. Xavier was standing in the doorway until he wasn't anymore—quick, like a camera flash. Then, the door slid back into place. The lock clicked, and the blinds were pulled back to their starting position, the individual slats turning to face inward, blocking me out. I screamed Xavier's name, once or twice, then the living room lights went out. It was so cold. I moved about the porch in search of another entrance to the house. There were steps descending into the backyard, but I needed my clothes. I thought about pressing my forehead up against the window when the phone buzzed to life in my hand, a nonstop stream of vibrations, icons popping up on the screen like threats from another planet. I looked down, unlocked the screen—the background photo: Ray and me, both of us doubled over with laughter at Edgewater Park, a small fire glowing next to us. I was so cold now, and lonely. I thumbed open my text messages and saw that Xavier had sent the photo to Ray, and Lucas, and Zeke. My finger slipped and the photo filled the entirety of the screen. I thought I was being sexy. The phone rang again, the vibrations burning my palm, and I answered without thinking, but I couldn't focus on the words being spoken to me, or about me in the background, I could only see my dumb, cartoonish face from the photo. And it was Ray, I was talking to Ray, who was yelling, slurring, and I wanted to tell him I was sorry, that I loved him, I've always loved him, but there was too much noise, and it was so cold, and the night was sinking away from me, and there was no way anyone would recognize me in that photo unless they were looking hard enough. I got it now. My lips were parted, eyes glazed over. I was gripping my penis in one hand, mid-stroke, and popping my ass out, cupping it with the other hand. I put in so much effort. I went for it. I gave everything I had.

What You Missed While I Was Watching Your Cat

The woman upstairs—have you met her?—moves furniture between 10PM and midnight. She drags what must be an anvil across the floor, and the whole apartment rattles. The Cat is not a fan. He stood on his hind legs, one night, balancing on top of the sofa, pawing manically toward the ceiling. Stretching until he was past my eye level. I rewarded him for his efforts with a healthy splash of a double IPA in his water bowl. Then I lit every candle you own—the scented Yankees and the waxy, white sticks that weep when they melt—and watched the Cat's shadow flicker and bounce around the walls, on the floor, against the windowpane, flashing in the corner of my eyes when I closed them, like the boogeyman from my childhood nightmares.

The whiskey you got me lasted a week. I rarely drink on Mondays, Wednesdays, or Thursdays; on a Tuesday, I killed half the bottle. Once I got a strong buzz going, I opened your dresser drawers, pulled out your boxers, bras, and panties. I held them against my groin and thrusted, hoping for a smidge of what it feels like for you two to have such close contact. Finished with the undergarments, I tossed them into a pile at the center of your bed. To see the product of your relationship reduced to these most intimate bits of fabric, all those tough, impossible-to-remove stains, and to fantasize about sixty or so of you in the bed, tangled up like a web of fitted sheets, with no cat to muck it all up—that was pure delight.

The Cat knocked over: a teacup, a bag of Doritos, library books, my toothbrush, a take-out container of dumplings, and your perfume and cologne bottles, which exploded like grenades all over your bathroom floor. The aroma made me so dizzy I draped myself over your bed and passed out for three hours. I woke to the Cat licking my face, his paw heavy on my throat.

Money is tight. This should come as no shock to either of you. I've never gone on a real vacation. Never been to Tokyo or San Juan, or London, or Tulum, where you two are now. It's hard to save on a salary that just covers the rent. I need another revenue stream, so I advertised a night's stay in your lovely one-bedroom, on Airbnb. Wanted to make a quick $75. One catch: the couple had to be OK with a man and his cat.

Then, yes, I lost the Cat. No idea how it could have happened—all the windows were closed, only one door into your apartment—but the Cat has his ways. I spent a night on my hands and knees, peeking under the couch and the bed, around your fridge; I arched my back like the Cat, ass in the air, chin to the ground, a prayer position. Clicked my tongue and called out his name. There was a pitter-patter behind me, then it disappeared in the walls.

One night, I posted up in your windowless kitchen, on the floor in front of the sink, to avoid the chaos outside. Gunshots in the alley. The metallic crash of trash cans hitting pavement. Yelling. Cursing. You left twenty cans of Fancy Feast, that good shit, out on the counter. I peeled back eight lids, a can for each day the Cat had been missing, and fed myself with a spoon. By the time the noise died down, I was flicking my tongue around the inside of each can to scrape up all the stuck bits. I was purring. I was becoming one with the cat.

The woman upstairs accosted me downstairs. She was lurking in the shadows of the staircase when I returned from work. Jesus, God, she said, your cat won't shut the fuck up. All day long with the wailing. It sounds like he's belting out the score to goddamn *Cats*. I looked at her, unsure how to react. The Cat is missing, I said, I don't know what you're hearing. It must be someone else's cat.

A dead cockroach tumbled out from under your bed one morning. It made a satisfying snap beneath my bare foot. I can't explain why, but I stood there for a while, grinding the roach into your carpet until my foot burned.

The Airbnb couple really got their $75 worth. They had sex in your bed. I'm talking Brazzers-style fucking: the headboard smacked against the window so hard I thought it would crack. I watched the whole thing perched atop a stool you keep in your bedroom, which after that night I realized you must keep around for this very reason, as a place for others to sit and observe you with stilted envy. I ate a bowl of cereal while I watched, barely getting the spoon in my mouth, all the milk and little marshmallows sticking to my cheek and chin. The couple finished up, settled into your bed for the night, and I excused myself to the kitchen, where I picked the marshmallows from my face and dropped them into the Cat's bowl. And then, of course, there was the Cat, crawling out from a cabinet, beaming up at me with his yellowed eyes. I cried. I reached to grab him in either a hug or choke hold, but he bolted into your bedroom and started screaming. Shrill, loud. The couple screamed with him. Together it had weight, sounded like a full choir.

Last night before you return, and it's just me and the Cat. I am sprawled out on your couch, taking up as much space as I can, and looking at the words in a book but not reading them. The Cat lands on my lap. I lower the book and see a tail dangling from his lips, the plump body of a mouse. Tomorrow, you'll feed him his food, clean his litter box. Next week, he'll avoid me when I come over for drinks. In a year, he'll fold himself beneath the couch when I'm around, lurk in the shadows. Won't care if I live or die. But right now, the Cat keeps moving, crawling up my stomach, my chest. I'm leaning back, my neck following the curve of your armrest, and the Cat keeps going. His front paws are pressing down on my shoulders, and the dead mouse is not even an inch away from my face, swinging above me like the blade of a guillotine, its delicate, pink nose, the tip of this loving gesture, the very thing that will break me.

Little Moves

In her will, Vanessa leaves Felix a collection of diet cookbooks, some missing entire pages, with the spines ripped clean off. Felix feels judged, now, looking at the stack of books. He had gained a little weight in recent years, but he didn't think anyone beyond his bathroom scale could tell. The cookbooks focus on trends in veganism, the paleo diet, and the weight loss effects of drinking citrus tea and doing yoga instead of snacking. One suggests he go about his day holding a single cherry in his mouth, wedged inside his cheek like a squirrel, so that whenever hunger strikes he can scrape the flesh away from the fruit and hide it in the cracks of his teeth. When it comes time for swallowing, he should experience a faint hint of cherry, which should, against all things he knows to be true, leave him satiated.

While flipping through the torn pages, he makes a point to eat a red velvet cake. The entire cake. Each bite is larger and sloppier than the last. In Felix's defense, the cake arrived along with several gray casseroles, muffin baskets, zucchini breads, and an edible fruit arrangement, which sits on a counter in his kitchen drawing flies to its juicy structure. And the cake, specifically, was sent from a coworker who once took him out for a drink. They had fooled around in the backseat of his car. Nothing too crazy, all of their clothes stayed on—although, hands may have slipped in between waistbands and asses were firmly cupped, but that's it. Honest.

The memory of that night is tainted: Vanessa would have disapproved of what occurred between Felix and this other man.

Anyway, there is a more pressing task at hand. Felix is now the designated caretaker of Vanessa's ashes. Life is full of little ironies. He knows nothing about what he should do with the ashes, but he hopes that it will be easier to care for the remains of Vanessa than it was to love her while she lived.

He calls Julisa, his living sister, for advice. Fortunately for Felix, Julisa cremated her Jack Russell Terrier three years ago. She pressed the button herself, a fact that soothes something deep in Felix's core.

"Well, the truth is I couldn't handle having them in the house," Julisa says. On the phone, she is loud, yelling like Felix is standing across the street and he needs to hear her above honking cars or those wild, thumping reggaetón beats of Saturday afternoon traffic. But this is always her way; he holds the phone an inch from his face as she speaks. "I tried putting him on the mantel, but it gave me the spooks. Ended up keeping him in the garage."

"But you don't have a garage."

"The last house did. Before the move, I buried him in the backyard."

"You dug a little plot for him? I guess that's lovely."

"I actually dumped the ashes into his favorite rosebush. I don't drive by the old house much anymore, so who knows if the roses still grow there. That bitch next door might have salted the lawn at one point." Julisa makes a noise, a cross between a hum and a snort.

Felix leans forward on the counter. His apartment complex lacks a garden of its own. There are some bushes out front, but they're often littered with Taco Bell cups and plastic bags crusted over with rainwater. Not exactly ideal.

"Look, I know I'm legally in charge or whatever, but, really, this decision should come from both of us," Felix says. "I don't want to screw this up or anything, and you and Vanessa were closer so you definitely get a say." Felix is sweating. He hasn't spoken this much about Vanessa in any capacity since the cremation, since he Slacked everyone at work that he would be taking two weeks off. He bundled together sick days and vacation days to make the time; HR only allotted three days for grieving. Over the week, he changed his mind—three days would have been plenty.

"You can count on me. Why don't I swing over for dinner tonight, then? We can figure it out."

"Tonight would be perfect, yeah. We'll make a plan, and then we can decide what to do with the box after. Or did you throw yours away?"

"Well, we got an urn. I kept it. It's on my bedside table, now, and I use it as a condom bowl. Tommy still gets to be around for the good times in my life, you know?"

"Dear God."

"It's what he would have wanted," Julisa says.

A moment of total silence stretches out between brother and sister, broken only by Julisa's soft weeping. Queasiness floods Felix's stomach. He abandons the cake. After harvesting all the cheesecake frosting, the remaining mound of sticky crumbs looks unappealing. He sees it and thinks about blood, about mealy earthworms writhing through his intestines, and then there is a flash of Vanessa's ghostly face in the hospital bed. The cancer, a slow crawl down her esophagus, had spread like jagged roots in her stomach. He drops his fork on the counter. It hits him: His sister is dead. So why haven't things begun to feel OK yet?

Julisa soars into a fit of laughter. "Oh my god, I'm kidding," she says. "I'm so kidding. I still got him in the urn. That's my baby. We keep him over the mantelpiece right under his portrait, you idiot, where the fuck else would he be?"

At first, Felix slides the box of ashes into the space at the top of his hall closet. But setting the ashes somewhere out of sight, as if he is embarrassed that his sister is dead at all, isn't quite right. It's not true that he's embarrassed of her death. He is, however, embarrassed of his apartment, how plain and poorly decorated it is, the lack of life in it. This is true of his closet, too. All the stark blacks and navy blues and charcoals, and the one mustard-yellow top he practically worships for its surprising existence in his wardrobe. Everything had been Vanessa-approved—clothes that are slimming and adult and masculine, shorts that cut off below the knee, tops that are presentable but not flashy, never flashy.

After flirting with the idea of leaving the box under the bathroom sink, and going as far as tucking it behind the toilet paper and closing the cabinet door, Felix decides there is no real choice here. The ashes belong on the coffee table. Equally visible from every corner in the living room. He can even see it from his tiny kitchen while cooking dinner.

Tonight, he chooses a recipe from Vanessa's least-terrible cookbook, *Latin Done Light*. The idea of doctoring up riced cauliflower with gandules and sofrito seems innocuous enough, but the tempeh guisado sounds like a high-risk-big-fail situation. He presses on. While the food bubbles on the stove, Felix peeks out into the living room and waves hello at the box. He wants a reaction, wishes Vanessa would jump out of the box. That she would scream and laugh, and immediately start criticizing his cooking and his most recent haircut, or the Mariah Carey and Jennifer Lopez he plays in the background when he's trying to throttle his anxieties. There is a footprint of movement in his body when the music plays, but he holds himself steady, doesn't allow his hips to swish, his body to roll.

He imagines Vanessa's hand on his ear as she points out the hole that never fully healed after she ripped out his diamond stud over ten years ago. And the sad part is, he knows that this would only be a start. An appetizer course. Then, she would really dig into him.

After dinner, Julisa curls up with a pillow cradled in her arms at the end of Felix's sofa. She is the aftermath of a downed bottle of Barefoot moscato. Her empty stomach, also a culprit in this mix. But Felix thinks nothing of Julisa's refusal to eat the dinner he prepared. Being able to cook for Julisa goes back to their childhood, when busy parents and a working Vanessa required him to bake off-brand chicken nuggets and frozen steak fries four nights a week. Tonight's concoction turned out to be a bland, soupy mess and, when Felix scraped the inedible meal into the garbage, it plopped as one mass from the plate to the bottom of the can. Felix saw the spillage and thought of gutted pigs, their entrails splattering on hot pavement.

In the living room, Felix opens a second bottle. He fills a glass to the rim, sets it down next to Vanessa's ashes, then together he and Julisa close their eyes, exhale. With glasses raised, they both make a silent toast. A quiet moment like this proves difficult. Felix wants to fill it with memories, fun memories, or at least somewhat happy memories, but for right now he can only swim in the cruelty of Vanessa's voice whenever she spoke to him, or about him, whenever she cocked her head to the side and raised an eyebrow because he had slipped, had taken a second to glance at an attractive waiter in a restaurant for too long, or when she traced the beeline between his eyes and Oscar Isaac's lips on the TV screen.

He and Julisa finish their minute of silence and each sip their wine; when Felix pulls the glass from his own lips, he wipes away a few tears.

"You know, looking at it now, in this lighting? Maybe the box could be a statement piece. A conversation starter?" Julisa offers.

"Oh, right, for the numerous cocktail parties I throw. And, hey, we can plate the deviled eggs right next to it. Perfect party." Felix runs his hand through his hair. It's been thinning for a good five years now. "That's the best idea you've had in a long-ass time." Julisa laughs, setting her glass down. "But, seriously, start inviting people over. Throw parties, if that's what you want. Hell, bring a goddamn date back here. Vanessa won't be around to judge him or her. OK? You're free to see whomever, Felix, and you deserve to be happy."

Felix nods his head three times, but doesn't say a word. He's not drunk enough to talk about dates, about love, about denying oneself such luxuries. If he got started, this would all lead to the coworker— Cristián, his name is Cristián—and in what world would he ever let Cristián into this apartment? Every decorative item or piece of furniture was selected under intense scrutiny, picked for the purpose of sanitization, to dissolve any unwanted personality traits. To bring Cristián, or Natalia from eight months ago, or Fernanda from a year before that, or Julián from almost two years after he first selected "Men and Women" on Tinder, or any of the fleeting relationships in his life before then, back to this apartment, is unthinkable, even now in the hour of Vanessa's death. It would be like bringing a date back to a vacant meat locker. Imagine the hanging frozen carcasses and the stench, all of that gone: a large fridge without the icy chill. Just a room, existent and open, but its truth scrubbed into oblivion.

"Perhaps I should move. Not sure where. Maybe rent a house in Lakewood," Felix says.

"No, you're not going to move. And, no, we're not done talking about your love life. That's always relevant information." Julisa slides over, closer to Felix, and pulls his arm around her shoulders. "Hey," Julisa says. "You got me, I got you. Remember?"

"Yeah, I remember. Right back at you."

It had been easy to tell Julisa. He hadn't given much thought to the specific words he had used at the time. Lucky for him, they jumped out, almost separate from himself. "I'm bi," he said, and Julisa smiled, leaning in for a hug like the one they're sharing now on his sofa. She thanked him for telling her, which so few people do, and there was no conditional I love you *anyway*, or *in spite of*, or a *no matter what*. Nothing but the unconditional "I love you." When Felix recalls this moment, he gets misty-eyed. He wanted to believe that at this point in his life the memory of coming out would be faint, like something from childhood that exists in fuzzy vision, viewed through a lens of hyper-nostalgia. Of course, this is a good memory. Very good. It's sweet and he is forever grateful for Julisa as a sister. But the reality is he's thought about coming out every single day since that first time with Julisa; it feels like thirst or hunger—palpable and gnawing, and thus far insatiable.

The drunkenness finally seeps into his limbs. It's scary to think about what it means to be open, to be honest. To be out. It's more than a chance to start over, or even begin at all—it's an opportunity to live each day unfettered by that shadow over his heart. What would he do?

Julisa pulls away from Felix and adjusts her glasses. She stretches, cracks her neck.

"So what are we going to do with this?" Felix taps the box with his foot. "She always wanted to retire in Arecibo. Do we pool together our money and fly out there? Dump the ashes into the water? Guess we should contact all the cousins. You know how much they loved her ass. Let's throw a big party. We'll get ourselves a fucking lechon, roast it on a spit, and maybe I'll get up on the drums with tío Osvaldo and join the jamboree. Fuck it, looks like she's getting everything she's ever wanted."

"Yes, I think that's exactly what we should do. And then maybe while we're out there, you'll meet someone, a hurricane relief worker, or a school teacher, and then you'll never leave the island either. And when we get older, I'll go ahead and join you."

"Come on, stop it already," Felix says. "Enough." He rises and paces around the sofa, holding both hands around the back of his neck. The heat in his face causes him to sweat.

"Alright, alright, Jesus. I didn't mean to make you mad. But, you know, this shit isn't easy for me." Julisa adjusts the hood of her sweater, fiddling with the drawstrings. She doesn't fully resemble Vanessa, but they share key features: their noses, for one, inherited from their grandmother, along with their broad shoulders and thick, curly hair. In fact, tonight is the first time Felix believes Julisa could be Vanessa's twin. They look so much alike, whether it's because of the apartment lighting or the angry tone in her voice; it's too much.

"Like, I get it," Julisa says. "You hated her guts. And I'm sorry, I'm so goddamn sorry. But come on, OK, I loved her like crazy. And I don't expect you to, and I'm not asking you to, but I did and I'm hurting here." She starts to cry, and while Felix would normally rush to hug her, he's paralyzed by how similar they look. He believes for a second that Vanessa has crawled out of the box and sat down on the sofa. If he were to touch her, there would be soot on his fingertips. Her body might collapse into a pile of maggots.

He remains standing, no longer facing Julisa. "Of course, of course. I'm sorry, Juli. Of course you're hurting."

For as long as he has despised Vanessa, Felix has carried only the deepest love in his heart for Julisa. And for years he thought that was enough, that as an older brother this was his only requirement. Siblings are difficult. They are not asked for and sometimes they are even unwanted. If he could love his sister, Felix always believed, that was enough to keep the relationship strong, but now, as he sits at the dining room table, behind Julisa, he sees the selfishness in this thinking. He had leaned on Julisa. What had he ever done out of pure kindness or love, for her? There is heartbreak caused by other people, those who are strangers until they aren't, maybe a person with whom a connection blossoms then withers into a past-tense state of existence.

But the heartbreak caused by family, by a sister or a brother, is more severe: they can absorb all the love and goodness you possess, drink it in like water, and keep on gulping it down out of ease, out of need, out of spite, out of bitterness. They can take everything you have to offer and leave your soul to dry.

Wanting to mend either of their wounds is not possible, Felix realizes, but there is tonight, this first real goodbye he and Julisa will say to Vanessa, and whatever comes after.

Julisa blows her nose into one of the pillows. The biggest one, with white and black frills. She's forcing it out, rubbing the fabric all up in and against her nose.

"You should know," Felix says, "Vanessa picked that one out."

This is enough to crack a smile on Julisa's face. She shakes her head, massages a corner of the pillow between her fingers. "God, she had shitty taste," Julisa says.

Felix considers his next words carefully. He doesn't want to lie, but perhaps there is room for some gray in his life, a blend of fact and fiction to get at the truth of his emotions. "I didn't always hate Vanessa," he says. He settles back into the couch, looks down at his bare feet when he sits, keeping laser focus on the black hairs on his big toe. "I guess that sounds like a *no shit, Sherlock* thing to say. But you weren't around then, and even when you did come along, things were still alright between us. You were a baby, so it sometimes felt like it was still the two of us."

"Felix, you're shaking," Julisa taps his knee. "Hey, we don't have to get into it. It's cool."

"I'll say this. Vanessa is the one who taught me how to dance."

"No shit?" Julisa is all smiles now. Felix knows this makes up for nothing, but this is where change can start. "But I haven't seen you dance, ever. Like, not even with Mami at her last birthday."

"Yeah," Felix says. "Well." He's not sure if there will be more crying, or if this is an attempt to avoid the breaking open of his own face, but he holds the expression. And then Julisa relaxes, settles into the sofa again.

"Hey, hey, I got you," she says.

There is no sleeping tonight for Felix. With Julisa knocked out in his room, he considers eating one of the casseroles. More eating instead of sleeping, instead of thinking. But for once, he isn't hungry. He reaches for his phone, clicks open the text messages. Cristián is the second-to-last person from whom he received a message. It's well past 3AM now, so Felix will wait until later, after the sun has risen, to reply.

The apartment is too quiet. He opens Spotify. He selects a playlist of old school merengue and salsa hits. The earbuds go in, and the music from his childhood, from when he used to dance, transports him. Vanessa had started dating when she taught Felix the right moves. Felix falls into the memory: their childhood living room, where the air conditioner wheezes in the window and flies twitch on ribboned glue traps. And there is Vanessa, moving like water to the music, total fluidity, and her first boyfriend, Ryan, lying across the sofa, his buzz cut tight, those "papi chulo" eyes, as she called them, gazing over at her as she moves. No one ever teaches a little boy how to one day dance with another man. Felix is looking at Ryan thinking he'd love to give it a try.

That's where the scene ends. What comes after could prevent this from being a happy memory. He'll cauterize reality, instead.

He stands and picks up the box of ashes. Holds it to his chest. And with the music steady in his ear, the vibration of his own eager heart, it all comes back: that instinctual swaying of his hips, legs moving to the rhythm. He circles the coffee table, the sofa, he moves across the room, raising the box higher and away from him, bringing it closer. That's how she taught him. Dancing was about bodies, about push and pull, about the separation and joining between two people.

And as Felix dances, the lid loosens, ashes sprinkling out onto his carpet. This goes unnoticed between the merengue and salsa numbers. He spins around and kicks and flails and doesn't stop on account of the ashes, which are falling, coating his coffee table and sofa. He doesn't stop either when Julisa emerges from his bedroom, screaming over the music blaring inside of him. Or when she grabs him by the shoulders and shakes him. He keeps on dancing, and swaying, and then he is singing, belting out in Spanish he doesn't fully understand, feeling light and free.

Unplucked

I go to the eyebrow artist, because no one else can give me what I crave: Chris Pine's sculpted brows. Beautiful, perfect. Thick enough to hold a smear of peanut butter, if I wanted.

Sarah told me the eyebrow artist collects hair from her clients in several jars, which she displays like a sepia-toned rainbow on a rickety shelf. The little strawberry blondes are kept separate from the chestnuts; the jet blacks shine in contrast to the dusty corns with their gradient of dull yellows. There were options here. I liked that. I could change my whole look. I could get white brows—a joke Sarah didn't laugh at. It's already bad enough, she said, why make it worse?

We're honest like that. I appreciate it, truly. From the bottom of my heart. Sarah calls me out when my shirt is wrinkled, or tells me when the guy I've been seeing for over three months is sleeping with the drug dealer who lives in her building. Ha! In turn, I tell her exactly what she doesn't want to hear, which is that she can't sing, doesn't hit any of the right notes, but beats them into something else entirely: a noise that is alien, unsonglike, unenjoyable to a blistering degree.

But—she makes each song her own in a way that makes me fear God. And there's something special in that!

The eyebrow artist prefers not to use tweezers or wax; she pinches the individual strands between her nails, rips out entire follicles so they don't grow back. This is ideal for Sarah. Her brows are flawless, highly arched. I told her I liked them, and she said, Not for you. She also warned it would be painful like nothing I had experienced before, which, when she said that, made me think of the firecracker incident last summer, the hell that snaked its way around my face and singed a layer of skin. My eyebrows and beard, eyelashes, ribbons of my neck—all gone. There might be blood, Sarah said. You might cry. And I laughed! I thought she was being dramatic. A little too concerned about my wellbeing.

Anyway, this was different. The hair would be stitched *into* my skin.

The eyebrow artist uses a sewing needle. The first puncture draws a bit of blood, which she dabs with a cotton ball. The pain is negligible. She's working magic on my face, giving me a self that isn't me, but the me I've always wanted to be. Isn't that beautiful?

Chris Pine was a deliberate choice, I tell her.

She nods and says, It's your life.

It is mine, so I describe how his brows compliment the rugged texture of his skin. Sure, he's blotchy in places, I say. It's not unappealing. In fact, he is comfort personified.

I don't tell her Sarah didn't approve at first. That she thought I should consider going with Daniel Radcliffe's caterpillars. Even suggested Jake Gyllenhaal's might be more *appropriate* over Chris Pine's. They weren't bad options. Plus, they were all far better singers than she could ever dream of being. I liked that.

After the firecracker incident, I spent my recovery time in the hospital staring at all three of their headshots, genuinely considering each shape of brow, their coloring. I wondered how these men might see *me* with brows like theirs. I imagined Chris, more than Jake or Daniel, would be the least creeped out by an eyebrow doppelgänger. Could maybe warm up to the idea. And Sarah, I decided, could deal. The eyebrow artist massages cooling oils into my brows, down my cheeks and neck. Everywhere she touches is still tender from the burns. I flinch at first, then settle into the tingling. Almost done, she says, and I don't want it to be true. I imagine the look on Sarah's face when she sees me. It might kill her! Which I don't want but would like for her to think about, to feel the intense gut-dropping sensation of confronting her own mortality in the face of mine. If you don't stop laughing, the artist says, we'll be here all night.

I try to push Sarah out of my head, but everything else is too funny: that drug dealer, who I later learned sold Sarah confectioner's sugar instead of the cocaine she paid for in cash. The fact that there was nothing between him and my ex. No messages to pull up, no proof. No meeting. But Sarah said it—she spoke it into existence. Sarah said it. How funny is that?

Turn over, the artist says, and I respond, Gladly. I face left then right, then left again, so she can get a good look, make sure there are no mistakes. These are Chris Pine's brows we're talking about. They deserve the best treatment.

She begins combing them upward to catch tiny flyaways, and I start laughing again. She sucks her teeth, waits a second for me to compose myself but it all goes full-belly. I'm wheezing, a clump of trimmed hairs caught in my throat. The look on the drug dealer's face, that was the funniest! Absolute confusion when I showed up to his apartment with a cherry bomb rattling in my hand. Sarah, fucking Sarah, had said, This will shake him up. This will show him.

The eyebrow artist isn't sure what to do when I flip from laughing to crying. My ears are ringing, I'm coughing so hard, and she is handing me tissues. No, no, it's fine, I say, and begin picking at the newly sewn hairs, so little and undeserving of this. I rip out a patch and know I'll keep going until they're stripped clean. Sarah said it wasn't the right style anyway, I try to say, I mean to say, but I can't form the words, can't understand what to do with the sound of my own voice.

Ordering Fries at Happy Hour

O.K., we'll get fries, it's done, it's easy, the menu offers lemon-parsley for $6 and $7 for truffle, so why don't we get the truffle, it's only a dollar more, a goddamn steal in this city, a hallelujah for the wallet, never mind that I had to hoist myself up onto the barstool, the seat of which couldn't hold a personal pan pizza let alone my entire ass, and never mind that when the fries finally come out, you'll look them over and say some shit about how we shouldn't be eating this, that fries are truly so so so bad, I guess we're being bad today, before mentioning that article from *The Atlantic* about the proper portion size of fries and suggesting we only take six fries each, which would leave behind a whole fucking basket, and then you'll laugh about the ridiculousness of it, the idea that anyone could stop at six, and then I won't laugh while shoving six fries, maybe seven or eight or ten if I can manage, into my mouth, and I wonder if fries have feelings, if it's cozy in my mouth the seconds before I grind them into paste, and do they feel safe in there from think pieces and Twitter threads and fat-shamers and coworkers who love happy hour but hate food, who never allow themselves to disappear into a bite, and do fries crave more than their salty graves, because sometimes I think, damn, what a joy it must be to live the short lifespan of a potato, and I think about their purpose, all that unlimited potential—we can mash or fry or bake or twice-bake or roast them in a hot oven or drown them in cheese—and if I were a potato, I gotta believe the best part is I wouldn't have to listen to you and the waitress argue over the chipotle mayonnaise you're ordering, whether it's an aioli or a remoulade, and I wouldn't have to hold back from finishing the fries before your dip arrives, and I wouldn't have to pause to count how many I've eaten, whether the six or eight or ten were *that* many more than the number you ate, if I got greedy, if I was being too much me again, or if you'd even notice, and there would be no waiting over who should eat the last cold fry, no, they would stay hot and crisp, and the oil on my fingertips would be a blessing, anointing my tongue with every lick.

Enough for Two to Share

When the bartender tells him the chicken finger appetizer is more of a meal than a snack, he slides over a stool and says, This guy. I'll share with you. And you think nothing of splitting a meal with a stranger, of intertwining greasy fingers. Napkins blotting crumb-coated lips so words can flow. Mastication: its own union.

He starts with his name, which you don't quite catch, later entering it into your phone under a single M. He says he works for an upscale restaurant an avenue over, handles their inventory, makes enough so he and his girl—so there *is* a girl—can hold onto the junior one-bedroom in Washington Heights. Says he's Puerto Rican, like yourself. He slaps you on the arm when he says it and you're all too eager to confirm the accusation. He hovers around you like burning incense. He speaks and the gentle smoke of his cologne comforts you.

The first round of drinks is a shot of Jäger with a Blue Moon to chase. So is the second, and third. The black licorice taste is an affront to your tongue, but burying disgust is a muscle you know how to flex. He dunks his chicken fingers good in honey mustard, crams four or five in his mouth at a time, chewing wildly. You hold back, swallow one before daring to grab another.

When you meet M, you've been in therapy for about three months. Got yourself a straight, affluent, white male therapist, which is hilarious because, against your better judgement, this means you spend each session seeking his approval. You hate that you've been conditioned to react in any way to the firm voice of a white man. You don't crawl towards him like a dog—you crave the pressure of his foot on your chest, wonder if he could stomp straight through to your heart, if he'd draw circles in your blood with his toes. He only ever wants to talk about your father, the gash created by his absence, so he can properly interrogate your everyday pain. You'd rather talk about love *now*, companionship *now*. There's a cockiness to the way he speaks to you: he withholds eye contact, reclines in his chair, both hands cradling the back of his head. What might you say to him about M? How, after two hours of drinking yourself dizzy and listening to him talk about the fights he's gotten into—over women, for women, with women, to spite women—you stay, order another round of drinks, charge it to your aching credit card. How you don't flinch when he says his girl hangs around with too many fags, or when he says no homo after grazing his knuckles across your knee. After the fifth round, you feel intoxicated by the pure liquor of his trust. You double over laughing and throw your arms around him for a hug, just a hug between dudes, friend shit, nothing gay about it, nothing at all, and make a temporary home from your cheek pressed into his neck.

You're a little funny, he says. Somehow you're both outside, and there is a cigarette between your fingers. The nicotine has you floating in place.

He asks if you've ever been in a fight. You don't grow up like us and not get a few scrapes. He avoids eye contact when he says it, releases the words into the night air, but you catch their meaning, the greater similarity that you share.

You tell M about the summer afternoons spent in your father's garage throwing your whole body into a punching bag. As a kid, you were predisposed to surrendering—a cause of great concern for your father who would scold you for picking female fighters in video games, for wearing pink in the summer, for sometimes skipping on the way to the park, as if such choices meant you were a sitting duck, vulnerable to hawks in the sky waiting to pluck you from the water with their hard beaks. He wanted you to know how to fight. You're too chicken shit, he'd say. Too much of a pussy. Beating the bag and bruising your forearms and fists against its leather was easier than conversation. While you threw punches, your father hyped you up until your arms went limp.

But it made you stronger? M asks.

I'm not sure, you say. But, I guess I'm here.

You once told your therapist that most nights feel like currents in a stream. That you wake the next morning disoriented, groggy from the rush. Tonight is a riptide pulling you under the surface. One moment you're outside the bar, watching M stomp a cigarette beneath his boot, the next you materialize in the frigid corner of an uptown A train.

M is telling you about his three kids. All boys. Different moms. They're spread out across the country. You imagine the dotted line: Los Angeles to Miami to New York, constellations of Latinx communities he tore through to wind up here. He's only close with the one kid in New York. Nine years old. Just celebrated his birthday last week, he says. He places a calloused hand on your thigh. Slides it through the opening in your shorts until it slips beneath the fabric of your briefs, cups around your balls. The air conditioning is blasting; the place where he touches you pulses with warmth. I've busted my ass for years to get what I got, he says. But nobody gives me credit. He strokes your shaft. No one, he says. He grips your dick harder and you squeeze your legs together, grinding down into the seat. When you come, your therapist's smug face flashes into your mind.

His apartment is exactly as described. Cramped, one bedroom. I know what you're thinking, he says. She's working the graveyard shift.

You hadn't stopped to think about the *her* of the equation and now it feels too late. M takes off his shirt, tosses it onto the couch. You remove your shoes, kick them to a corner, and begin unbuckling your belt. This is all so routine. When you first started meeting strangers for sex, you wondered if maybe you were doing it all wrong. If maybe you didn't *have* to meet them in the middle of the night, quietly, tiptoeing down unlit hallways to bedrooms in a whisper, something easily ignored. And now there is the faint footprint of the woman in M's life. Dehydration curls around your lips—your lick them and run your tongue along your teeth, catching a hint of grease.

M pulls you in, and you're ready for a kiss. Ready to cross the line into new territory. Kissing someone discreet? Disrupting his relationship with your body? Are these the right questions? your therapist will ask.

The kiss is delicate, tender. Not at all what you expect. Men in their forties and fifties have been kind to you, treating you at times as something fragile, at risk of shattering. But men in their thirties, like M, tend to be rougher with you, and a bit cruel. They often look past your humanity when given the opportunity of a quick nut. And when they're thinner, your body becomes their personal plaything: a doll that can be flipped and pressed down, splayed open on command, a handheld Hoover vacuum at their service.

Hey, M says, his hand around your neck. You tense up at first, then give into its heat. The rough edge to his skin is soothing. Could you? Well, could you punch me here? He places your hand on his chest. As hard as you can?

The first punch demands nothing of you. Like this?

Yeah, he says. But harder. I'll tell you when to stop.

And so, you hit him. Again, then again. Harder each time until pain radiates up and down your arm and his chest is slick with sweat, the hair matted. You keep punching. Skin to skin, a knuckle into the meat of his pec. You switch to your left hand when the right goes numb. He tears up, he grunts—the noise is piercing, like a bark. And the satisfaction of making another grown man cry floods you. Sometimes you need to let it out, your therapist would say. Sometimes you need to let it go. See? How does that make you feel? Right now, you need to center yourself. There won't be a tomorrow. Only tonight. The room is unsteady, heavy around you like the deep end of a pool. You're drained, flaccid. You crave fresh air in your lungs, an escape from the apartment funk. But you need to hang in until the end, don't you?

Finally, M falls back onto the couch. The skin on his chest is hot pink, steaming. You take a deep breath. Exhaustion is a sagging weight, but you continue to stand.

You're game for anything at this point, aren't you?

You've made it this far.

Keep it going.

Sit on my face, you say.

M doesn't hesitate. He's on his feet, sinking into the couch, and then you're working your way between his legs, the cushion sticking to your back. Above you, M is fire. M is shade. Your tongue is wet, eager.

I think we both needed this, he says.

He lowers his ass to your mouth; you open your lips.

Yes, yes. There you go. There you go.

The Secret to Your Best Self

Three minutes into Marcos's workday, the Keurig craps out. It sputters, it cries, it refuses to perform. Marcos has been known to kill six K-Cups in any given afternoon, so this derails his whole day. He doesn't even like the mud that comes out of K-Cups—he's really a stovetop Bustelo man—but he is in no place to turn his nose up at free coffee. He can't slip out between meetings to buy a cup of tar from Starbucks, a break-in-case-of-emergency situation that would follow him like shame, the burnt-coffee stench clinging to the fabric of his sweater. In the evening, he returns home, severely decaffeinated, with a mild pain pooling in his temples. And instead of winding down, swapping out a crisp collar for a threadbare T-shirt that once belonged to his ex, Ramón, Marcos is wired up for his first cup of the day.

He begins his pursuit by pacing around his kitchen, sticking his head into every cabinet. He finds a can of whole coffee beans, which are perfectly useless. No spice grinder! He opens the fridge and leans way in, almost folding over himself when he pokes his head between the economy-sized jar of pickles and a water pitcher, its insides peppered from an expired filter. No coffee. Oh, but why shouldn't there be a problem? Of course, of course—his roommate, Xiomara, hides the ground coffee in her bedroom. That's where she keeps all the goods: the coffee, the boxes of white chocolates her mother sends around Christmas, packs of facemasks she bought on a trip to South Korea, a silk robe she wears after showering. She started locking her bedroom door after Ramón left.

Marcos frees himself from the fridge as a stronger pain throbs inside his head. He wishes now to stick a bendy straw in an entire carafe of fresh coffee. How he longs to suck! He wants the black coffee to coat his throat, burn it, to brew in the barrel of his stomach; he wants to rile up that loyal acid reflux, get it to skyrocket and explode. The possibility of this acidic diet successfully eroding the remaining lump of his heart is slim—but he chooses to believe.

In the kitchen, there are six cabinets. One is full of mugs. Mugs from New York and North Carolina, from his alma mater, gift shops along highways in the middle of who can even remember, and the ones Ramón had bought as birthday presents for Marcos in his early twenties, each one hand-painted with phrases that make little sense. Things like: "Here Is How I Rise," or "You Would Have to Be the Fool," or "Tango in the Dark, Waltz in the Light," or "Can, Will, When." Are they aphorisms? Obscure mantras? Marcos has spent every morning since the breakup mulling over them at the sink, rolling the mugs between two soapy hands, waiting for the hot water to reveal a clearer meaning.

He grabs one now that reads "The Secret to Your Best Self." Perfectly incomplete.

He slams the mug down on the countertop, enjoys the feeling of ceramic shattering in his hand. Motivated, he reaches for a cabinet door and yanks it off the hinge, tossing it across the kitchen like a Frisbee. And so it goes: the five remaining cabinet doors meet the ground, faux-wood scuffing tile, the edges peeling back to a surface of decay. Then the decorative pieces on the counters, the walls: a ceramic spoon-clock, fancy bottles of vinegar and jars packed with dried herbs, a duck-shaped cookie jar, a once-used mesh strainer. Everything soon lies scattered about the kitchen, in shards or dented beyond repair. The drawers follow: out tumble cutlery and rolls of aluminum foil, Ziploc bags, soy and hot sauce packets. Marcos's headache intensifies, and when he glances down, he realizes he is holding a steak knife. He massages the grooves of its wooden handle as if it possesses the ability to grant wishes. There are only two options: puncture the source of highest pressure in his head, or slash through the walls.

But before he can do either, he hears the click of a lock and turns to see that Xiomara is home from work. When she finds Marcos with a knife in hand, a manic terror in his eyes, Xiomara clasps her hands together. Inhales, then exhales. They've been here before. For weeks, well, maybe it was months after the breakup, Marcos would sneak into her room after work and steal her silk robe. He enjoyed the cold fabric on his skin, the touch of *something*. Xiomara would discover him passed out on the sofa hours later, white chocolate chips all over his chest, melted into the robe and on the cushions—and Marcos, snoring, lulled into a sugared slumber.

In silence, Xiomara removes the knife from his grip then grabs the can of whole coffee beans off the counter. She takes from it a handful, letting the beans roll from her palm onto a cutting board, the only utensil not on the floor, and Marcos watches them like marbles circling each other, unsure if they are following or trying to outrun one another.

Xiomara slices the beans, going in for a rougher chop until they resemble little mounds of dirt, like the piles left behind when repotting a plant. She grabs as much as will fit in the crook of her fingertips and inches them close to Marcos's mouth. He does not hesitate—he opens wide, allowing her to sprinkle the coffee dust onto his tongue. The headache does not wane, nor does he feel revived. The coffee tastes bitter; without any liquid, the residue leaves his tongue feeling raw. But over time, as he sweeps the kitchen, listening to Xiomara talk about her day, about everything other than the mess around them and all that he's destroyed, he stops tasting the coffee. And the craving dissipates. And he stops missing what he cannot have.

That Version of You

I've been trying to feel more comfortable in my skin. *Let go, man. Don't think it, do it.* That's what everyone's been telling me. Not you, but everyone else.

The club thumps with Britney, Carly Rae, and Sia, and they all got my body loose. To feel this good on the dance floor requires space in my stomach. The last meal I ate: a bowl of Raisin Bran, a cup of oat milk. Lapped up every drop so I'd have enough to hold onto without feeling weighed down. I'm starving, but this way, I can keep up with you. Except—you're doing the Straight Guy thing. Again. You're bumping against any woman who gives you an opening, and some who don't. I'm not intervening; I watched you drain an entire vodka Gatorade on the train into Manhattan, your stomach empty, and the last time I got involved, my nose made friends with the back of your hand.

A guy approaches me to dance when Whitney comes on, and I will myself to stay cool about it. When he leads me to the dance floor, I spot a touch of gel on his eyebrows. I'm guessing it's meant to keep them in place, which I get on a practical level; we're all trying to tame the untamable. I smile, which elicits one from him, making his face look like sculpted wax when we step into the wrong lighting. And there's plenty of wrong lighting tonight.

There's a good chance you're hooking up somewhere. I assumed before leaving the apartment that I'd end my night abandoned, cooling off in the backseat of a Lyft, fantasizing about taking your clippers to shave a clean stripe down the center of your skull while you sleep. We've joked in the past about you hating my guts and me wanting you dead. Some nights, this cuts closer to the truth.

I dance a few songs with Gelled Eyebrows until La Roux starts up—then he asks if I'd like a drink, which I do, but you're disappearing through the side door and I know I should check on you.

In the alley, you're kicking a dumpster, really laying into it. So now, tonight is more like that time in college when I found you on the floor of our common room, in your boxers, hours after ditching me at a house party. You were eating cheesy bread from Domino's, which you'd recently told me *I* should stop eating because of the cholesterol, but when I knelt down to touch your shoulder and connected with your eyes, pink and glazed over from Everclear and Pepsi, you offered me a warm piece, the white cheese stretching away from the box like taffy. Tonight, I'm dealing with that version of you.

You start going on about how women don't like shorter dudes, as if it's a fact, how it's all about your height, how your dance partner took off with a six-foot-tall guy, maybe taller, with good hair and nice jeans, and how could you ever expect to compete with someone like that? I've been hearing the same tale since we were both nineteen and held toxic beliefs about what we thought women owed us.

Anyway, you say, wanna get some food?

Gelled Eyebrows is behind me, waiting to be introduced. Before I can ask him his name, you kick the dumpster one more time and say, Fuck it, there's a bodega a few blocks away from here. Gelled Eyebrows and I exchange a glance, his eyebrows in full slants of confusion. I clear my throat and think maybe I should take pity and let him go, but then I nod your way, and soon he's following me following you.

We stand in line at the bodega, our faces lobster red, hair soaked, shirts damp and yellowed under the low-wattage fluorescent lights. Gloria Estefan's voice hovers around us. And I think maybe the rhythm *is* going to get us.

We approach the front of the line and I can almost taste the grease hissing on the griddle. I'm drooling, starved. I got my mind on bacon and globs of cream cheese doused in hot sauce. Gelled Eyebrows squints at the menu. I guess this is a bad time to tell you I'm vegan, he says, and you roll your eyes.

I'm thinking about a salad, you say. Doesn't that sound nice? Your eyes are bloodshot now and you're wavering with the rest of the crowd. I want to shove your face down onto the hot griddle, creating a beautiful sizzle. But no dressing, you add, though we didn't ask. I stopped messing with that shit like a month ago.

More people pack in and our noses almost touch the deli case. I'm keeping centered with my palm on the glass; its grimy surface feels like our entire world.

We pay for our food and step back outside. The air is cooler. Gelled Eyebrows slows behind us. He says, This has been, well, something, but I'm heading home.

Are you sure? I ask, though I lose interest before he answers. He shoves both hands in his pockets and the two of us are caught in a stalemate, which you break by holding out your salad container, saying, Actually, do you want this? There's no cheese or anything and I'm not hungry anymore.

No, not really, Gelled Eyebrows says. He pulls out his phone to request an Uber. I'm OK. Get home safe, he says, then he leans in for a hug, and I'm so surprised by his kindness I don't wrap my arms around him. He pulls away, offers a pathetic wave as he crosses the street. I feel a pang in my chest watching him go. I had derailed his entire night, dragged him out to this bodega all so I could put off the inevitable— when the night loops back to you and me.

When it's just you and me, I don't think about our differences. We're two short kings. And that scares the shit out of me. How easily I can fall in step with you. How safe this friendship feels when it's just us, until we're in a room with other people, surrounded by more interesting narratives, and I begin to pick myself apart. I get too caught up on everything about me that doesn't match up with you that I can't fully *be*.

The street is emptying out. I consider my sandwich. I rip open the aluminum and stare at two beautiful halves, the layers so delicate and perfect: white cream cheese, chewy bacon, a ripple of red hot sauce. Life is rarely this beautiful. The steam rolls up, tickles the inside of my nose and I drink it in, let it work like sage on my spirits.

You gonna eat it or make out with it, you say. You're standing closer now. I imagine smashing the sandwich into your face, can taste the satisfaction of smearing cream cheese into your hair and burning your nose with hot bacon. But I offer you one half of the sandwich instead. And without another word you receive the offering, raise it to your mouth, and bite.

I'm Not Hungry But I Could Eat

I'm finishing up a falafel I picked up after work when I get Valeria's text. She's going through it and asks if I'm free to catch up at the diner we both like. It's been a few weeks since we last saw each other and shared a meal, and I know *going through it* is code for *something with work, something with the family*. I lick white sauce from my wrist, text back that I'll see her in twenty. For friends, I make time. For best friends, I make room in my stomach.

Valeria doesn't need to see the menu. She orders grilled cheese with tomatoes and mushrooms. She skips the fries, which means she'll pick a few from my plate; I order a chicken club then change my mind and ask for the buffalo chicken sandwich with extra sauce.

So it's like this, she says, and begins describing her situation. She works for a ghoulish startup that approaches people in hospice care, offers to handle the writing and finalizing of their last wills. Some days it feels like I'm forcing their hand, she says. The patients are so over the process. I sometimes write outlandish, freaky shit into the document and they sign off without pause, then go right back to their morphine drips and sponge baths.

I'm trying to be a good friend and engage in active listening because the job sounds brutal, but I'm feeling terrible, physically, and getting shifty in the tight squeeze of our booth. All that extra feta and garlic whip I ordered with my falafel is starting to hit. And I've dairied my coffee to hell.

We stop talking when the server arrives with our food. We like this place because the portion sizes are always huge, like a dare. When the server leaves, Valeria claws at my fries.

I mean get this, get this, Valeria says, stabbing the air with a bendy fry. Last week, I finally snapped and slipped in a line about this guy leaving his skin to his son. Not the snakeskin boots he told me to include, oh no. His entire skin sack.

Jesus, I say, and force down a bite of sandwich. Good flavor, but the breading is impossible in my mouth. Is it too late to fix it? I ask.

Oh, and tell on myself? Absolutely not, she says. It's been signed and sealed and it'll be known in the next forty-eight to seventy-two hours, anyway, so good luck to that family.

She reaches for another fry, so I lift my entire plate. Take as many as you'd like, I say. I tip the plate over onto hers and watch all the fries slide into their rightful home. Then I swallow the last bite of the first half of my sandwich and regret it. I poke my stomach with the back of my fork, see if I'll pop. I can't shake the idea of receiving loose skin, I say.

Doesn't it sound heinous? Like, we know you're grieving, but please take your loved one's former casing. Valeria finally breaks into her grilled cheese though by now it's lost its stretch factor. Also, the guy was on the heavier side so, you know, it's a lot of skin.

I peel the breading from the second sandwich half, ball it up. It's so dry it crumbles, leaving my fingers stained red. I imagine all of my skin spread out on the floor. OK, it's a lot. The size of a king-size comforter. I think about changing my diet and losing weight, the alleged potential of doing so. If anything would change. If life wouldn't be more or less the same, but with a new character design, clothes that fit properly, new muscles. Maybe, possibly. But what would it do to me? Valeria holds her mug up to a waiter for more coffee and I do the same. I will always accept more. I order more wings during happy hour, or another bowl of pierogis piled high beneath a thick dollop of sour cream when it's late and we're drunk and Valeria isn't ready for the night to end. I eat cheese by the brick. I drink beer and wine until my bladder descends and I'm ready to burst. I'm built to be a glutton. To take in, and expand. To get full and loose in the mouth and house the booze sloshing in my stomach until the bar is closing and it's time to part ways, say goodbye to the bartender, another temporary friend, another connection I've held onto for several hours, by consuming, ordering more and more, by filling up a space.

I say, I'd leave you my skin. I don't make eye contact when I say it; Valeria falls silent. She finishes her sandwich and I do the same. The last bite is all dense bread, but I swallow it anyway.

Valeria thanks me for listening. I ask if she's looking for work elsewhere, tell her I could put in a word at my office if she needs it. We're not hiring, so it would mean nothing. But it sounds like the right thing to say.

She runs her hands through her hair, pulls it back into a messy bun. I think I might get a slice of coconut pie, she says. It's fabulous here. You interested in sharing?

I'm at the kind of full where it hurts to breathe. Another bite is another step up a staircase. Valeria makes eye contact and I can see how exhausted she is. We got a lot more to discuss. I finish off my coffee, feel it thick and cold on my tongue, and pick up my fork again, ask, With extra whipped cream?

Only if that's what you want, she says.

Half Hearted

Michael never asks if Hector is OK or how his day is going or even if he is well; instead, he asks, "How is your heart?" The first time Hector encountered this question, he and Michael were sipping wine from plastic cups, their lips puckered and red. Afraid of explaining the floating in his chest, Hector answered with a lie: "Well." Three months later, when he was asked again on the chilly top of a Ferris wheel, Hector answered with a little less restraint. "Weak," he said. "Like it's giving up." All around them, the park was a cluster of lights and polyphonic music. Michael's shaggy hair danced in the cold wind as he nodded along to Hector's talking and talking and talking about the difficulties of walking around with only half a heart.

Hector believed the awkward moments of his formative years could be traced back to his incomplete interior. The boys and girls he lusted after all told him he hugged coolly, without any firmness in his embrace. Photographers described his smile as "crooked" or, strangely, "disingenuous," the point being he lacked an evenness in his presence. The first time Hector had sex, he rolled over onto his side after coming, his body dotted with sweat, shocked stiff. Hector stared into the wall for hours, while his partner lay next to him, confused and quietly hurt.

He told almost all of his later lovers about the half heart. But no one accepted his words as fact. "No, it doesn't beat slower than a whole one," he would have to say. "It's still a heart like yours. It fills me with blood and gives me life." And still, whomever he was dating would press their fingertips to his wrist to compare the frequency of their pulse against his. He would then shake his wrist free and breathe in, hoping that if he held enough air in his lungs he could put off crying until the man or woman would disappear from his life forever.

Things between Hector and Michael weren't horrible before, but after the night on the Ferris wheel, all the magic in their relationship disintegrates. There is another dinner or two, followed by drinks in Michael's neighborhood. They make several trips to a bookstore together, where Hector watches Michael linger in the same aisle each visit, picking up a book by an author he's read but who isn't his favorite, and slipping it back onto the shelf before they leave. One day, a moving truck delivers Michael and all of his belongings to Hector's neighborhood. Hector understands he should be filled with joy or at least a faint happiness, but when they walk to the local restaurant to celebrate, he does so nearly half a block behind Michael. At dinner, Michael makes an attempt. He reaches over to stroke Hector's knuckles, but Hector pulls away, resting the untouched hand in his lap for the remainder of their meal.

After his breakup with Michael, Hector fears his heart might devour itself. You lose what you don't use. When this idea morphs into a source of panic, Hector searches online for a doctor who specializes in matters of the heart.

The specialist he finds is a septuagenarian with a full head of hair. The existence of all that hair, the fullness of it, comforts Hector, and he decides he might be able to trust him. In the sessions, they address Hector's anxiety and the constant fluttering in his chest. He describes the emptiness of his heartbeat. He mentions Michael with both eyes desert dry.

One afternoon the specialist asks, "Do you miss Michael at all?"

Hector slides as far back as he can in his seat, his spine conforming to the chair's padded arch. "I don't know if I'm capable of missing someone," Hector says. "I think I'm missing out on what it must feel like to miss him."

"So you're numb?" the specialist presses.

Hector massages a spot on his chest. A dull ache pulls downward, settles in his stomach as a hard ball. "Maybe this is what it feels like to miss him?" Hector asks. He folds his arms and his eyes dip toward the gray carpet, stained in spots of yellow and a concerning blue.

The specialist flips to a clean sheet of paper in his legal pad and starts sketching a heart. Hector assumes the drawing will be of an anatomically correct one, but the specialist executes the symbolic shape with perfectly symmetrical slopes at the top, an even point at the bottom. "You know, few people are actually wholehearted. It's more common for people to either have three-fourths of their heart intact or one-fourth," the specialist says, lopping the sketched heart into sections with a fat Sharpie.

"What about half?" Hector asks. He unfolds his arms, and then traces over his chest with his free right hand.

"Not as common," the specialist says. He frowns and passes the legal pad to Hector, who receives it like a sword, palms pointed up, the pad balancing on his fingertips. The lines he sees inside of the heart are mangled, some areas denser with black ink than others, a bunch of jagged riffs. He studies the sketch for a few minutes, imagining the various ways in which his heart may have been split in two.

"If you'll let me," the specialist says, "we can crack open your chest. We can determine the severity of your condition." Hector considers the offer; he sits, listening to the clock ticking, a desk fan, the whisper of traffic outside, his mangled heart. "We may not be able to make your heart whole again, Hector," the specialist says after too much silence. "Close to whole is all I can promise."

Before the anesthesia overtakes Hector's consciousness, the night of his breakup blinks fresh in his mind. He sees it from above, from the perspective of a drone hovering feet away from their passenger car. The subconscious has little interest in observing Hector and Michael, so it flies lower, catching sight of another couple seated in the car directly below them. These lovers are exchanging open-mouth kisses, sloppy with smacking noises. There is heat and passion between them. It is clear from this slice of their anonymous life that neither carries a defective heart. Hector wonders if maybe they were more worthy of sitting at the highest point of the park, and then he slips into a medicated sleep.

The specialist pries his fingers into Hector's chest cavity. He peels back the folds of skin, scrapes away pockets of yellow fat, revealing the cavernous lump of a half heart. His assistant shines a light on the mass. Going into the operation, the specialist knew he would never be able to suture together a false half. He knew only more problems would arise with such an irresponsible solution, some new condition to taint Hector's quality of life. With the pulsating organ settled in the palm of his hand, the specialist discerns at least two chambers, almost all the meat still intact. His assistant taps him on the shoulder, flashes the light closer to the heart's surface along its rough edges where the muscle is shredded. And there, the specialist sees the pulpy meat of two remaining chambers. Though not complete, Hector has within him the elements of a whole heart. The specialist works quickly. He ignores the blood, dark and thick upon hitting the air, spurting out of

Hector's chest. He ignores Hector's heartbeat, which fluctuates when the specialist rotates the half heart, when he connects a broken valve and applies pressure to the cavity. He ties the loose ribbons of veins and arteries together, pulling them into a tight, sinewy bow, so that what was once a grotesque half heart is now a solid muscle. Once the surgery is done and the assistant finishes stitching Hector's chest back together, the specialist feels confident that he has done his absolute best to salvage Hector's ability to love.

During recovery, Hector moves from his bed to the bathroom, then to the kitchen where he prepares a simple meal of oatmeal in the morning or bland stew in the evening, and back to bed, where he collapses and sleeps without dreaming. He checks his reflection in the mirror every day and tries to remember if life was always this hollow, that perhaps what was fixed was never really broken.

"Opening yourself up and examining what's on the inside is never easy, Hector," the specialist says over the phone. They speak once a week. "Change can begin if you want it to, but now it really is all up to you."

Unsure of where rehabilitation should begin, Hector goes back to his very beginning. He listens to the love songs his parents played when he was a child, hoping the boldness of their love for one another and for him will heal him. He burns music onto CDs and plays twelve tracks in one sitting, memorizing the lyrics like a password to accessing a fuller life. He takes up an online cooking class. Following along with the woman on the screen, he chops up raw meat for a zesty steak tartare, and he minces jalapeños and garlic for salsa. These acts of normalcy, according to the specialist, will remedy the past twenty-five years of an abnormal existence.

When his heart regains some of its strength from the music and his body is rejuvenated by an enhanced diet, he walks. If the day is snowy, he leaves a single set of footprints in the path that loops the perimeter of his apartment building, and by the time he returns from wherever he had wandered off to, the footprints are dusted over again. His journeys never take him too far. There is a coffee shop about two blocks from where he lives, in which he sips tea and finds comfort in the clickity-clack of other customers' computers. He avoids bookstores, but often will visit the library, a rotunda bursting with the rustling of pages and whispers of gossip. He feels now for perhaps the first time in his life no awkward glances coming his way, nobody suspicious that inside of himself he contains only a negative space.

Today, Hector walks to the grocery store behind his apartment, the one with wide windows and intimidatingly long aisles. It is there, in the midst of a frenzied voyage for free samples and frozen burritos, Hector's cart hits the back of Michael's leg. Hector expected, in the way all broken-hearted people do, that if he ever ran into Michael again he would see him and question why he was attracted to Michael at all. He would think that there was no reason for missing him. But suddenly Hector is warm, flushed with thoughts of Michael and Michael and only Michael: his carnival laughter; how every morning he would greet Hector with a coffee-stained kiss; the way Michael spreads peanut butter on both halves of the sandwich to prevent the soft jelly from leaking out the opening between the crusts; and his belief that floating could be a beautiful thing. The memories ripple through him, fresh and exciting, but he knows that this Michael was always there. It was Hector who had been unable to meet Michael's willingness to love with equal openness.

Now, Hector watches Michael open the freezer door. He watches him reach far into the back and pull out a pack of black bean and cheese burritos. "I thought you said these agitated your stomach," Hector says. No formal *Hello* or awkward *Hi there*.

"They do," Michael says, now looking Hector in the eyes. He laughs and places the frosty pack of burritos in Hector's shopping cart. "They're your favorite, aren't they? I was getting them for you."

Hector's chest tightens. Michael loosens the grip on his basket handle, which tilts from a balanced center more severely to the right. Then he says, "Hector, I'm happy to see you. I've missed you so much these past few months. How is your heart?"

Hector wants to say this: living isn't easy. On his worst days, it feels like breathing through a paper bag, waiting for someone to rip open a hole. But he decides to say, "My half heart still aches and probably always will." What he can't possibly know is that Michael's whole one feels twice the aching. Michael nods his head and Hector thinks he is going to apologize for the pain before the two go their separate ways. Instead, Michael loops his fingers through Hector's, leads them to his wrist. Hector thinks, *Who's to say that neither of us will be destroyed by this?* Hector closes his eyes. He is waiting to feel the stark difference in their pulses. He believes Michael's will feel more complete, but after a full minute, the beating feels exactly the same. And still, he fears that Michael's heart may become half before his whole. Or Michael might remain intact while Hector disintegrates. But in feeling Michael's pulse swell under the touch of his thumb, he swears to himself that he can learn to cradle the heart of another inside of his own. And isn't that reason enough to try?

Here's the Situation

Here's the situation:

There's a guy, Danny, sitting on our stoop. He's got his face in his hands and he's tapping his left foot, slapping the heel against our bottom step, counting down the seconds until he loses his shit.

He's waiting for Eduardo.

Like all the others.

Here's how it started:

In high school, Eduardo picked up a new guy every few weeks in the spring, every couple of days in the summer. He let his dick rest through the winter, for cuffing season. Sometimes I tagged along on the dates— I'd sit on a bench in the park, staring out at the little creek while they sucked each other off behind a group of trees. I never participated or anything freaky like that. Not that Eduardo ever invited me to join. But he needed to keep me close. For all the good times, he said, and especially the bad.

Here's the situation:

Danny has always greeted me with a smile, toothy beyond what I deserve. When his late nights with Eduardo started folding into Saturday morning breakfasts, I set my alarm to wake hours before either of them would stumble out of Eduardo's room. I whipped up tall stacks of blueberry pancakes twelve weekends in a row. The three of us sipped café con leche at the kitchen table, our forks dripping with syrup, feet bare, hair messy. I lost full days to the haze of those slow mornings, each one stretching out like a long, delicious nap.

Here's how it often plays out:

I go up to the guy and sputter out any name, say, "Andrew?" (This is not strategic at all on my part. I'm rarely told their names.) The guy then cocks his head up at me like I'm trying to start a fight. "Helios," he might correct me. Coldly, that's how he'd do it. I then tell Helios-Andrew-Sergio-whatever that our friend Eduardo won't be back anytime soon. I might toss in a detail about a month-long vacation, a family emergency, his mother found dead on the side of a street, his brother taking a bullet in the back, a blood transfusion needed that only Eduardo could fulfill, and that in light of these events, instead of occupying space outside my apartment, it would be best for the man to go.

The good ones, the guys for whom I feel the most, do leave. They take the hint and disappear.

Here's the situation:

Danny, wearing Eduardo's college hoodie, leaning against his door, waiting for him to finish up with a work call.

Or Danny, curled up with a book at the end of our sofa, the early morning sun dissecting him through the blinds.

Or Danny, alone at our kitchen table, half-past 2AM, a bottle of blueberry wine drained, sitting in silence, chin in hand.

Here's what I've learned:

There is power in ending a relationship. Even the ones that were never yours.

Here's how it can go bad:

They sit for too long, faces cupped in hands, the sun sinking down on us. They get indignant. Say something like, "He can't just do me like this," or "Nobody has the balls to break it off in person anymore?", or "Who the fuck are you?", or "No, really, who the fuck are you?", or "Then why are you so fucking smiley about it?" They often scan my face for permission to scream or run away, but I never stay long enough to see what they decide. This is for the best. I squeeze past them, wedge myself between their slumped body and the stoop railing, through the door and straight into my apartment, where I start a pot of coffee and wait, in the darkness, for Eduardo to come home.

Here's what I remember:

Our classmates fawning over Eduardo. And why wouldn't they? He could roll his Rs better than anyone could. When he danced bachata and merengue in the school gym, he moved across the floor as if it had been waxed just for his feet. I was good for a dance, maybe two, if my partner didn't mind my taking a breather every couple of songs, and I spoke both English and Spanish with a lisp-y tongue, the words coming out wet and scrambled.

Here's the worst it's gone:

Helios-Andrew-Sergio-whatever got into the apartment. I had been preparing dinner, a stew bulked up with potatoes and carrots. The chef's knife was on the kitchen table. I imagined him getting there first, holding the blade against my throat. But I was quicker: I blinked and saw the flash of red—how easily the blade passed through his stomach, like popping a water balloon, all the tension breaking away.

Here's how the last guy left it:

"He'll never love you."

Here's the situation:

Danny raises his head from his lap. He says, "Eduardo isn't returning any of my calls, Mateo. Do you know what's up?" I consider a pre-packaged reply, or backing away and running around the corner. I could lie and lie and lie again.

Here's how I sleep:

Here's the situation:

Danny is sitting on our stoop. His frown could draw blood.

Here's what I miss:

When we were kids, I would strap on a pair of retro roller skates and Eduardo would let me tether myself to his bike. I weaved over asphalt and brick-paved roads behind him. While we sped through the city, the air scraping against my face, I felt like a kite not quite catching the wind, thinking that if he could go just for a little longer and if I tightened my grip, I might take flight.

Here's the situation:

I will hand Danny a bag of groceries, invite him inside. I'll slice open a loaf of bread, slather its fluffy interior with butter, toast it, and serve it alongside strong Bustelo. We'll sit together at the table, Danny and me, and hold each other in place until Eduardo walks in through the door.

Then, together, we'll let go.

Tag-a-Long

Cynthia invites me out to join her work friends in the East Village. Some crowded dive bar where the clientele works in new media and slugs happy hour-priced well drinks all night with a wink-wink of irony. I love it. I'm trash for it.

We're here because Cynthia wants to make her final move on a coworker she's crushed on for six months. His name is Aiden. I know, because she types it out as "A*den" in our chats. A secret between the two of us. I wonder if there was time she might have typed my name out like "Y*diel," if I was ever her secret to share.

A*den hasn't arrived yet, so we link up with her friends. One is a twink journalist who was nominated for a GLAAD award for an article he wrote about living on the A Train for 72 hours straight, riding it back and forth between 207th and the Far Rockaways, shitting into a diaper, eating one single sandwich for the duration of the whole trip. He says hello then drifts off into a crowd forming at the back of the bar. The other friend I've met once before. I can't remember her name. She is a newish hire at their company. She writes literary-themed quick hits for the site, like "10 Books to Read When You Just Can't" and "6 Novelists

Who Are Secretly Republican." We attempt small talk but the bar is so loud and my hearing is shot. I nod my head through conversation, accept any word she says as fact. *Something something* yes sure *something something* I've heard that too.

I turn back to where I think Cynthia is standing, but she's gone, slithered away to find A*den. Great, fine. No, no, it's cool. I slide into a booth across from the quick-hits writer, who I guess has known me long enough to bring up her current dating troubles—a difficult guy, a quiet guy, a guy who isn't picking up what she's been putting down.

Yadiel, she says. (Not Y*diel.) Am I hopeless?

I drum my fingers along the side of a beer can. I don't know. Maybe, I say. Maybe not. But that's not an answer, not a good one anyway. She asks about my love life, which I hate, because the answer is *no one* or at least *no one who is available or interested* and so *nothing happening there* and a silent plea for us to drop it. She asks if I'm on the apps, and I say yes, duh, what choice do I have? I split my time between Tinder and Grindr like any other bland bisexual. She laughs when I say this and I don't understand because that wasn't a punchline. Dating is pointless, I add, wishing I had a second beer to crack open, for the drama of it more than anything, for the flair. It's all a game, a frustrating one with no clear end in sight, like the Sims, like Animal Crossing, though at least in those games you can make friends; you can become a god for plucking a turnip from the earth.

Well, at least you have double the options, she says. Both men and women? The words fall from her lips, so easy, so careless.

More options, yes, I agree, but what I mean is more chances for someone to say no, more faces for me to scroll past, who also scroll past me, still so many people with whom there is no connection, no electricity or zing, no desire to reach out and touch beyond the physical. More options, sure, I say, but no results.

Across the bar, I spot Cynthia. A*den is laughing with a fat mouth and I want to feel glee for them. I want to cheer them on. I want to understand that this is a good thing. I purse my lips, point with them until this friend of my friend leans forward to get a view, too. She smiles, and so I follow suit.

Then Cynthia brings A*den to the booth. She slides in next to her friend and A*den remains standing. A *choice*. I'm not sure what he has to prove. The booth is now too crowded. Perfect time for the GLAAD award nominee—not winner, important to remember—to drop down next to me. The friend of my friend nods in his direction now, as if to say, *look! an option, look! go for it.*

The nominee pulls out his phone, scrolls through Grindr. He pays for premium; I know because he's sorted his men by ethnicity and is specifically looking for Latinos. I checked the app before we entered the bar and now see my face pop up on his wall of options. I slide my phone onto the table, thumb open Grindr and find his profile. He identifies as a dominant piggy top, devil-emoji, hot-face emoji. He wants a hungry bottom. Looking for now! Looking for no games! Just sex!

Cynthia and A*den are deep in conversation, awkwardly so—he's so tall he has to pop a squat to be at eye level with her. What if we both got lucky for once, is a thought I have, then I tap the flame icon on the nominee's profile to feel a jolt of life. I watch as he clicks open mine.

Last week, a man invited me over, waited face-down-ass-up with a condom on his nightstand. We fucked until it stopped being fun twenty minutes in. Two weeks ago, there was a date with a woman at the Hooters near Penn Station. We shared a sloppy meal, fine conversation, then she left a $0 tip and I carried on with the date for another three hours anyway because I was out of my apartment for once, I was out with a woman for once. Last month, there was a man who catfished me, sent photos of someone thinner, fitter, then met me at the door with only a ski mask and a build like mine, which would have been fine but I left because it felt like the reasonable thing to do. I needed to make some kind of decision, even if it led me back to square one.

Across the table, the friend who's name I should remember is stirring the ice around and around in the bottom of her cup. Hopeless, huh? The nominee machine-gun messages me three ass shots back-to-back. Dominant piggy verse-style. He's concentrated on the phone screen but gives nothing away, whether he knows the chubby bottom of his dreams is sitting next to him, his for the taking. Upon closer inspection, each ass shot is taken from an angle that makes my spine itch. I block him. I'm just as hopeless.

Then, Cynthia starts kissing A*den. Finally! And I'm happy for her, I try to remind myself, I am. This was the goal of tonight; this is what she wanted. And so, as her friend, it's what I wanted for her. But this guy, this A*den, shows no enthusiasm. I'm fascinated. She's got him by the face and he doesn't move. She runs her fingers through his hair and he doesn't bend. Here, without overthinking it, I extend a hand across the table toward my new friend, embrace the weight of hers in mine, then I tilt my head back toward Cynthia, and together we watch her place a hand on A*den's chin, open her mouth wider to release her tongue.

The piggy top taps his foot, shaking the table. He sets his phone screen-side down and sighs, deeply, all the air from his mouth stale and hot, souring the ecosystem of our booth. I'm going to get a drink, he says, and leaves without offering anyone else another. A*den opens his eyes, annoyed at our existence, and scans the table, locks into a staring contest with the woman holding my hand. She tightens her grip, I do the same. It's instinct. It's the most natural act in the world.

Around us people chatter, laugh, sip out of plastic cups, spill sugary drinks onto a sticky floor. They're in the moment, grooving to a humble base of music too low to fully appreciate. We should disappear, I think, but the *we* of my thoughts no longer includes lip-chewing, triumphant Cynthia. I squeeze my hand again and quick-hits faces me, raises her eyebrow. I nod toward the door, though I have no game plan for what happens next. Food, maybe more drinks.

This could end in friendship or heartache, or both. It's always a little of both. I slide out from the booth and she follows, slipping beneath the table and crawling over the seat to escape. When she reappears, her hand is back in mine. Behind us, Cynthia is in heaven. But A*den is a statue, a rock. A creature from another world. I mean, a whole other person has attached herself to him—why, then, has he done nothing to pull her in?

Juan, Actually

Juan is mulling over what Carla said at the party about not fearing death when his Lyft driver bodies a cyclist. Actually, it's a delivery guy. A working man. Juan sees two plastic Have a Nice Day smiley face bags wrapped around the handlebars before he sees the body, its legs unnaturally splayed out on the pavement, an arm tangled in the front tire's spokes.

The street is empty. At almost 4AM, there is only the wind, the background roar of cars along the main stretch three blocks away, and the Lyft driver screaming, Shit. No, no, no. God, no. Please, no. Not again.

Juan leans on the car for support. He's never encountered a limp body like this. He watches the driver kneel down to check the delivery guy's pulse; he listens to the driver count, the seconds coming out in huffs.

I'm calling an ambulance, Juan says. He struggles to retrieve the phone from his pocket. There's so much blood mingling with the chow mein and shrimp fried rice that exploded onto the pavement—Juan is having a hard time.

The driver is up; he slaps the phone from Juan's hand. Help me get him into the car, he spits. We'll handle this.

Juan's immediate thought is, I'm not giving this man a tip. I'm not paying him at all. Maybe he'll get my first one-star rating. But the driver's glare is persistent, fire fueled. Propelled by the urgency of the situation, Juan joins him on the ground. He pulls the delivery guy's arm free from the spokes, and all those thoughts of annoyance, of *come on really? how did we end up here?*, are replaced by the mild, steady rush of white-hot fear.

Where had the night gone wrong? Surely, this was Juan's fault.

The party had been on a rooftop. Carla's twenty-seventh birthday. Not a huge milestone—no Hallmark cards with a particular snark about the big 2-7 available at CVS, no new legal status unlocked—but seeing the other side of another year feels like an accomplishment when the world is burning. At 10PM, she said it the first time: I'm not afraid to die. Someone in the group who drinks too much and is motivated by an ugly need to one-up everyone replied, That's truly the wildest thing I have ever heard.

Then, at 1AM, Carla whispered the words again to Juan. He smiled, finished his second IPA; the hops weren't as bitter as he expected. He had always admired Carla's bravery, which he attributed to her Leo rising and Leo moon. He followed her lead whenever possible. Since college, they had acted insufferably rather than authentically. But they had done so together. The togetherness was key.

Seriously, Carla said. I'm not scared of dying. The act of it, the reality? I'm not scared to say goodbye to this world.

Blood isn't quite gushing out from the delivery guy's head, nor does Juan consider it sluicing, but there's still a flow. Actually, it's making a mess all over his lap, the entire backseat. Is it dickish to send a Venmo request for the $10 minimum Juan pays at his neighborhood wash-and-fold? He cradles the delivery guy's head, presses his hand to a clump of sticky, matted hair, and mentally deducts the amount from the Lyft fee.

The delivery guy's mouth opens and closes, like a suffocating fish. He looks young, maybe teen-aged, way too young to be working this late, and yet. Life is filled with so many *and yet*s. Juan says, You're going to get through this, you're going to be O.K., which he doesn't believe, not even a little.

The driver speeds down side roads and squeezes through narrow alleyways. Keep him awake if you can, the driver yells, give him a shake. Don't let him slip away. His eyes flicker between the road and the rearview mirror, to Juan.

He's going to be pissed about his bike, isn't he? Juan asks. They had left the crumpled frame on the sidewalk. Tossed it onto the curb like trash, like nothing.

The driver looks ahead. Let's not worry about that, he says.

How many cyclists have you hit? Juan asks. Is this like a *thing* for you? Have any of them died?

They approach a red light and the driver raises the volume on the radio.

Toward the end of the party, Juan had been relatively sober. His choice. He watched Carla dance with her girlfriend Sophie against the backdrop of a flashing neon deli sign. It soothed him.

Their swaying, their happiness in the moment was overwhelming. Infectious. Juan could have giggled to himself, but then he would have been *that guy* at the party, instead of that *quiet* guy. What stuck out to Juan wasn't that Carla was happier than he was—no, actually, that was part of it. It made him sad, all too self-aware if he focused on it. But he was happy *for* her, even if on the surface he was tripped up by the idea that Carla thought nothing about opening her life to Sophie. She barreled forward without any doubts holding her back: she liked Sophie and told her as much and the two entered a relationship, emerging as a couple. Juan blinked, and there they were. Juan blinked again, and he hadn't moved an inch.

The blue-black sky passes on all sides of the car. The Lyft driver blows through another red light and a few stop signs, past a group of drunk white people stumbling toward the train. Some are exiting their own Lyfts and Ubers, their destinations exactly where they expected. When the driver cuts off someone else on a bike—this one a non-working cyclist who doesn't topple but manages to throw up a middle finger and a *Go to hell, fuckwad!*—Juan inspects the car's backseat, which is only enough room for three bodies if two of them aren't already bleeding. He slides a thumb to the delivery guy's throat to check again for a pulse, and he considers his own life, the blood-pumping pulp of it. He's always lived like he's strapped to a conveyor belt headed for some obvious inevitability. Of course, he likes to think he takes risks: he walks home from the train at 2AM with music blasting through his headphones, a hoodie pulled over his head—a moving target. He visits C-rated diners and orders the calamari. He sleeps with men who hide their faces, buries all of his vulnerability inside their slick warmth, quickly and recklessly, unprotected, because it's exciting, because it can feel like a game, because sometimes a shock to the system is necessary for enduring. But, otherwise, the march toward death is slow. Lonely, actually. That Juan runs toward it feels like the result of a programming error, especially now, as the delivery guy begins crying out. Vibrations shoot up Juan's arm into the thick of his chest. If he is afraid of death, of dying, every possible act of it, shouldn't he be unafraid of the opposite? Shouldn't he be doing all he can to run in the other direction?

After all the guests had left, Juan smoked a joint with Sophie and Carla. He hardly ever smokes, but this was a special occasion. Sophie showed them both a new kind of high that involved taking a hit then leaning back over the roof's lip. They were to hold the smoke in until after their heads were fully dangling over the edge and the city appeared upside down, and all the pressure had built in their noses and eyes and ears, and they felt a kind of drowning without water, a total submersion in the night chill, until releasing the smoke became an involuntary action.

The delivery guy is screaming when the Lyft driver opens the backdoor. Doesn't stop when the driver reaches for his legs; Juan continues to keep the delivery guy's head in place, pinned down to the seat. The delivery guy flails and kicks in all directions. They are parked right outside the Emergency Room, so close to the entrance Juan might laugh. He could spit and hit the revolving doors. If we could just roll his ass through those doors, Juan thinks, if we pounce on him, wrestle him into submission, and strap him to a gurney, this whole night will have been worth it. Why else would Juan have stayed along for the ride? Wasn't this his choice?

Sophie and Carla had managed their hits better than Juan had. He coughed, his eyes stinging, the red pigment in his skin rising to the surface. He rushed to sit up and the city flipped around. All the blood flowed into the rest of his body; his arms and legs buzzed back to life. The stillness within him had snapped in two. And he felt like he was spinning in place, slowly, all zero gravity in his hands and in his head, his heart rotating on an axis, like he would never know the comfort of a stable world again.

Carla kept her head craned over the edge. Her face flushed pink. The veins in her neck and forehead swelled up. And Sophie, a trooper, held her position at Carla's side. I could stay like this forever, Carla said, finally, releasing the smoke in a glorious ring.

And, actually, Juan wished he could too. But once he stood and saw Carla and Sophie with their hands joined, he felt like he had been putting off the rest of his life. It was time to leave.

The delivery guy's foot cuts across the driver's face, his elbow meets Juan's mouth, which fills with hot blood, a loose tooth. The delivery guy falls forward onto the asphalt, then picks himself up, screams louder, more fearfully than in the confined space of the backseat, and he breaks off into a run around the corner, away and away. Gone. When the sound of his footsteps dissipates, relief overcomes Juan.

Fucker, the driver says. We try to save him and he doesn't even appreciate it. He doesn't understand what we did, what we didn't have to do. We were great, he says, and Juan is stuck on the *we* of their night, the city turned upside down within it. We're heroes, dammit, the driver says.

The driver steps away from the car, his hands on his hips, mouth hanging open to welcome the murky dawn. Juan walks up to the driver, pulls him in for a side hug. They don't stand there to watch the sun break open the sky. They don't get back into the car and complete Juan's original ride either, though later, when Juan wakes around noon, he will wonder about all the million ways that could have played out, if they had crossed the finish line together. But for a hug, at least, and the moments after, Juan is fine with being blood-stained and sweaty. Tired. Banged up, just a little. Not defeated in any major way. Not looking down when he should be looking up, or looking backwards. Actually alive.

Publication Credits

Thank you to the editors of the publications who gave homes to earlier versions of some of the stories from this collection:

Queen Mob's Teahouse: "That Version of You"
BULL Men's Fiction: "Packed White Spaces"
Little Fiction: "Better Than All That"
Cosmonauts Avenue: "The Secret to Your Best Self"
Lunch Ticket: "A Mountain of Invertebrates"
Wasafiri, Issue 98: "Little Moves" in a slightly different version titled "They Can Leave Your Soul to Dry"
Pidgeonholes: "Unplucked"
Okay Donkey: "Ordering Fries at Happy Hour"
Third Point Press: "What You Missed While I was Watching Your Cat"
Pithead Chapel: "Half Hearted"
The Forge Literary Magazine: "I'm Not Hungry but I Could Eat"
jmww and *Forward: 21st Century Flash Fiction*: "Here's the Situation"

Acknowledgments

Thank you to the SFWP team, especially my editor, Monica Prince, who saw me and the work I was putting out into the world. Had you never asked about my manuscript, this collection would have remained a Google Doc I'd tinker with endlessly for years and years, I'm sure.

Thank you to my core writing group: Maureen Langloss, Sara Lippman, Alice Kaltman, Shayne Terry. Every workshop was a masterclass; a good chunk of this book would not exist without your love and kindness.

Thank you to Ashley Lopez for reading this book and taking a bet on what comes next.

Thank you to the staff of Giorgio's of Gramercy: Brock Underhill, Jordan Centeno, Alisha Hawkins, Matt Summers, Amy De Stefano. Stretched-out happy hours under your care gave me the space to mull over these stories.

I am always here to make friends, so a full-hearted thanks to the following souls (writers, editors, and non-literary folk alike): Marie Solís, Marcos Gonsalez, Tyrese Coleman, Danielle Bukowski, Jean-Luc Bouchard, Delaney Fischer, David Garfinkel, Jenny Feldman, Penny Luksic, Ashley Pecorelli, Mark Meneses, Laura O'Dea, Olivia Wolfgang-Smith, Jude Wetherell, Catie Iannitto, Pete Iannitto, Rachel Menth, Henry De La Cruz, Ashley Burdin, Raven Leilani, Sydney Jeon, Michelle Foytek, Erin Murphy, Melissa Campion, Jocelyn Tiller, Meghan Phillips, Matt Mastricova, Cameron Moreno, Jaime Fountaine, Tomas Moniz, Melissa Ragsly, Dina L. Relles, Aram Mrjoian, Lauren Dostal, K.B. Carle, Tyler Barton, Anna Vangala Jones, Amy Stuber, Becky Robison, Amy Rossi, Patrick Mullen-Coyoy, Roy Guzmán, Danny Caine, Ruth Joffre, Megan Giddings, Aaron Burch, Bryan Washington, Suzi F. Garcia, Dan Hoyt, Leonora Desar, Nicole Steinberg, Ruth LeFaive, Kelsey Phelps, Monet P. Thomas, Natalie Kay,

Jennifer Fliss, Josh Denslow, Foster, Michael Tager, Chelsea Fonden, Hannah Grieco, Derrick Jefferson, Chris Molnar, Sarita González, and too many others.

A special thank you to my Barrelfam: Becky Barnard, Dave Housley, Erin Fitzgerald, Tom McAllister, Mike Ingram, Dan Brady, Tara Campbell, Matt Perez, Joe Killiany, Christina Beasley, Sheila Squillante, Killian Czuba, Yohanca Delgado, Siân Griffiths, Sam Ashworth, Susan Muaddi-Darraj. Thank you for welcoming me in and giving me a literary home base, for teaching me how to have fun with writing, for filling my stomach with ungodly volumes of bourbon and my heart with endless joy.

Thank you, and all the love, to my family: my parents, Eunice and Onix Garcia; my brother and sister-in-law, Mario and Ivette Morales; my nephews, Javier and Dominic; my grandparents, Yolanda Giusti, Clarixa Garcia, and Luis Gonzalez.

If we ever shared a meal or got sloppy over drinks together, I thank you sincerely. A night spent with someone is a night not spent alone.